THE WORLD OF
NORM

Thank you to my fantastic agent, Lucy, and my editor, Catherine, for having such great taste. Thanks also to Philippa and Anna at Scottish Book Trust – and a special mention to the unstoppable force of human nature that is Maggie Gray from Fife Libraries.

ORCHARD BOOKS
338 Euston Road, London NW1 3BH
Orchard Books Australia
Level 17/207 Kent Street, Sydney, NSW 2000

First published in 2011 by Orchard Books

A Paperback Original

ISBN 978 1 40831 303 9

Text © Jonathan Meres 2011

The rights of Jonathan Meres to be identified as the author and Donough O'Malley to be identified as the illustrator of this work have been asserted by them in accordance with the Copyright, Designs and Patents Act, 1988.

A CIP catalogue record for this book is available from the British Library.

7 9 10 8

Printed in Great Britain

Orchard Books is a division of Hachette Children's Books,
an Hachette UK company.

www.hachette.co.uk

THE WORLD OF
NORM
MAY CONTAIN NUTS

JONATHAN MERES

ORCHARD

To Max, Ollie and Noah.

Without me — none of you would have been possible.

CHAPTER 1

Norm knew it was going to be one of those days when he woke up and found himself about to pee in his dad's wardrobe.

"Whoa! Stop Norman!" yelled Norm's dad, sitting bolt upright and switching on his bedside light.

"Uh? What?" mumbled Norm, his voice still thick with sleep.

"What do you think you're doing?"

"Having a pee?" said Norm, like this was the most stupid question in the entire history of stupid questions.

"Not in my wardrobe you're not!" said Norm's dad.

"That's from Ikea that is," added Norm's mum, like it was somehow OK to pee in a wardrobe that wasn't.

Norm was confused. The last thing he knew he'd been on the verge of becoming the youngest ever World Mountain Biking Champion, when he'd suddenly had to slam on his brakes to avoid hitting a tree. Now here he was having to slam on a completely different kind of brakes in order to avoid a completely different kind of accident. What was going on? And what were his parents doing sleeping in the bathroom anyway?

"Toilet's moved," said Norm, hopping from one foot to the other, something which at the age of three was considered socially acceptable, but which at the age of nearly thirteen, most definitely wasn't.

6

"What?" said Norm's dad.

"Toilet's moved," said Norm, a bit louder.

But Norm's dad had heard what Norm said. He just couldn't quite *believe* what Norm had said.

"No, Norman. It's not the *toilet* that's moved! It's *us* that's moved!"

"Forgot," said Norm.

Norm's dad looked at his eldest son. "Are you serious?"

"Yeah," said Norm, like this was the *second* most stupid question in the entire history of stupid questions.

"You *forgot* we moved house?"

"Yeah," said Norm.

"How can you *forget* we moved house?" said Norm's dad, increasingly incredulous.

"Just did," shrugged Norm, increasingly close to wetting himself.

"But we moved over three months ago, Norman!" said Norm's dad.

"Three months, two weeks and five days ago, to be precise," said Norm's mum, like she hadn't even had to think about it.

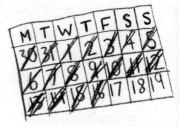

Norm's dad sighed wearily and looked at his watch. It was two o'clock in the morning.

"Look, Norman. You just can't go round peeing in other peoples' wardrobes and that's all there is to it!"

"I didn't," said Norm.

"No, but you were *about* to!"

Norm's dad was right. Norm *had* been about to pee in the wardrobe, but he'd managed to stop himself just in time.

Typical, thought Norm. Being blamed for something he hadn't actually done.

Norm considered arguing the point, but by now his bladder felt like it was the size of a space hopper. If he didn't pee soon he was going to explode. Then he'd *really* be in trouble!

"Go on. Clear off," said Norm's dad.

Norm didn't need telling twice and began waddling towards the door like a pregnant penguin.

"Oh, and Norman?"

"Yeah?" said Norm without bothering to stop.

"The toilet's at the end of the corridor. You can't miss it."

Norm didn't reply. He knew that if he didn't get to the toilet in the next ten seconds there was a very good chance that he *would* miss it!

CHAPTER 2

Norm tried every trick he knew to get back to sleep. The trouble was, Norm only knew one trick – counting sheep jumping over a gate – and it just wasn't working. For a start he'd made the gate much too high. There was no way a sheep was going to be able to clear it. Not without some kind of springboard or mini trampoline, anyway. In the end there was a big pile-up of sheep, all milling about like...well, sheep, basically. It was so annoying. And the more Norm thought about it the less sleepy he got. And the less sleepy Norm got the less chance there was of carrying on the dream where he'd left off. Was he destined to become World Mountain Biking Champion or not?

Norm was desperate to find out.

Norm tried to guess what time it was. The last time he'd looked it had been 2.30. That seemed like ages ago. But it was hard to tell. It was still pitch black outside. A couple of cars had driven up and down the street and some random guy had wandered past, singing tunelessly at the top of his voice. Norm opened one eye to check. The red digits of the digital clock glowed, suspended in the dark.

2:33am

Norm couldn't believe it. Three minutes? Was that *really* all it had been since he'd last looked? Three measly minutes? A hundred and eighty stupid seconds? A twentieth of a flipping hour? No way, thought Norm. That can't be right. The clock must be faulty. The battery must have run out. The world must have stopped turning. There *had* to be a rational explanation. It couldn't possibly have been only *three* minutes! But it was. He was never *ever* going to get back to sleep at this rate!

It didn't help that Norm could hear his dad, snoring away like a constipated rhinoceros. Not that Norm had ever actually heard a constipated rhinoceros – but he imagined that's what one would have sounded like. He'd never noticed how loud it was before. Before they'd moved house, that is. Their 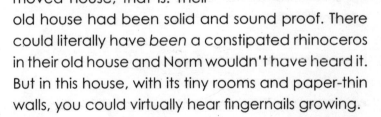 old house had been solid and sound proof. There could literally have *been* a constipated rhinoceros in their old house and Norm wouldn't have heard it. But in this house, with its tiny rooms and paper-thin walls, you could virtually hear fingernails growing.

Norm tried putting his pillow over his head but it didn't make the slightest bit of difference. It was an incredible racket. It wouldn't have been so bad,

but his mum and dad's room wasn't even next to Norm's! How come his mum could sleep through it and yet Norm couldn't? How come his stupid little brothers could sleep through it and yet Norm couldn't? It was just so unfair, thought Norm. But then so was everything these days.

Like being blamed for peeing in his dad's wardrobe for instance. Or rather, *not* peeing in his dad's wardrobe. How unfair was that? It wasn't Norm's fault they'd moved was it? It would never have happened in their old house. In their old house he'd never once woken up to find himself about to pee in anything *other* than a toilet. In their old house Norm would have been back to sleep ages ago!

The more Norm thought about it, the more wound up he got. Why on earth did they have to go and move in the first place? Who in their right minds would leave a nice big house for a glorified rabbit hutch? Well, not exactly big.

It wasn't like it was massive or anything. But compared to this place their old house was like Buckingham flipping Palace! It just didn't make sense to Norm.

And yes, Norm *knew* there were homeless people out there who'd give anything to have a roof over their heads and that he shouldn't be so ungrateful and all that stuff. His mum and dad didn't need to tell him *that*. Just like they didn't need to keep banging on about starving children in Africa every time he left a bit of broccoli, but they still did. If they were *that* bothered why didn't they just bung it in a jiffy bag and send it to them?

And how was Norm ever supposed to become World Mountain Biking Champion eating flipping broccoli anyway?

By now, Norm was oozing anger. The air around him practically crackled, as if he was some kind of human electricity generator. Never mind flipping wind-farms or solar flipping panels. If harnessed correctly, Norm could have single-handedly powered a small town for a whole year!

It was probably just as well then that Norm *didn't* hear Brian, his middle brother, pad along the landing and open his parents' bedroom door. It was probably just as well that he *wasn't* there to see Brian lift the lid of the laundry basket and pee in it. And it was *definitely* just as well that Norm *didn't* see Brian pad away again without so much as a peep from his parents, one of whom was still snoring like a constipated rhinoceros and the other of whom was busy dreaming of her next trip to IKEA.

A car drove down the street, the beam of its headlights flickering through a crack in the curtains and briefly illuminating Norm's face. But amazingly, Norm never even noticed. Like a hurricane that had finally blown itself out, Norm had fallen fast and furiously asleep.

The *good* news as far as Norm was concerned was that he picked up the dream exactly where he'd left off. The *bad* news was that his best friend Mikey became the youngest ever World Mountain Biking Champion. Norm came second. It was *so* unfair.

CHAPTER 3

Norm gradually became aware of the sound of muffled voices. What on earth could his mum and dad be talking about at this time? It was the middle of the flipping night! Surely whatever it was could wait till morning couldn't it?

Norm opened an eye and looked at the clock.

10:14am

Norm closed his eye again and snuggled back into the duvet. By now he was beginning to make out occasional random words and phrases like *stainless steel*, *dishwasher friendly* and *twelve easy monthly payments*.

His parents really should get out more, decided Norm.

The fog of Norm's mind slowly began to clear. Something didn't quite compute. Something wasn't quite right. But what?

Norm sat up and looked out the window. It was light outside.

Funny, thought Norm. How come it was light in the middle of the night? Was there like an eclipse or something and nobody had bothered to tell him? He wouldn't be surprised. Nobody bothered to tell Norm anything. It could literally be the end of the world and Norm would be the last to find out.

Norm opened an eye again and looked at the clock.

10:15ₐₘ

The penny still didn't drop immediately, but when it finally did, it dropped with an almighty clunk. There wasn't an eclipse. It wasn't the middle of the night any more. It was actually the middle of the morning. It looked like Norm *had* got back to sleep after all!

"Aaaaaaaaaaggggh!!" screamed Norm, leaping out of bed.

There was a sudden rush of footsteps up the stairs. By the time Norm's mum appeared at the door, Norm was in his pants and hopping round the room trying to put his socks on.

"Are you OK, love?" said Norm's mum in a tone that suggested that at the very least she'd been expecting to find Norm lying in a heap on the floor, possibly even gushing blood.

"No, I am *not* OK, actually!" said Norm. "Why didn't you wake me, Mum?"

"Because it's Saturday," said Norm's mum, matter-of-factly.

But Norm wasn't listening.

"How am I supposed to get to school on time if nobody wakes me? It wasn't *my* fault I overslept! It wouldn't have happened if we lived in a *proper* house! How am I supposed to sleep with that flipping racket going on? Honestly, it's a miracle the neighbours haven't phoned to complain! Mind you, they don't actually *need* to phone do they? They can just shout!"

SHUT UP!

neighbour

Norm stopped, but only because he needed to breathe. His mum just smiled, which somehow made Norm even angrier.

"I'm serious, Mum! The walls are so flipping thin you can hear a spider fart three rooms away!"

Norm's mum laughed.

"It's not funny!" said Norm.

"I know it's not, love."

"So why are you laughing?"

"Because it's Saturday, Norman."

 said Norm.

"It's Saturday," said Norm's mum. *"That's* why we didn't wake you."

"You might've said."

"I did."

Norm looked at his mum for a moment.

"Is this a wind-up Mum? It really *is* Saturday?"

Norm's mum smiled again.

"You don't honestly think we'd let you sleep in on a school day do you, Norman?"

It was a fair point, thought Norm. His parents were weird, but not *that* weird. It really *was* Saturday.

Norm felt both relieved and happy. Not only was he *not* late for school, he didn't actually have to *go* to school! And as if that wasn't brilliant enough, Norm suddenly remembered that Mikey was coming round to bike! Things just didn't get any better than that!

"You can go back to bed if you like, love," said Norm's mum.

"Where's everybody else?" said Norm.

"At the supermarket," said Norm's mum.

Norm looked puzzled. "So – who were you talking to just now?"

"Nobody."

"Yeah you were," said Norm. "I heard voices."

"Shopping channels," said Norm's mum.

"Shopping channels?" said Norm.

"Yeah."

That explained the random words then, thought Norm. He might have known. His mum was buying more and more stuff off the telly these days.

"Well?" said Norm's mum, expectantly.

"Well what?" said Norm, even though he knew perfectly well what that particular *well* meant.

"Aren't you going to ask me if I bought anything?"

Norm knew his mum would tell him whether he asked or not. He might as well get it over with.

"Did you buy anything, Mum?"

"Set of saucepans."

Norm looked at his mum. "But..."

"But what love?"

"We've already *got* saucepans."

"Yes, I know. But it was a bargain!"

"Yes, but we don't actually *need* any more saucepans, Mum."

Norm's mum looked at Norm with an almost pitying expression. "No, you don't *understand* Norman. It was a *bargain!*"

Norm's mum was right. Norm *didn't* understand. Why buy something just because it was a bargain? What was the point if you didn't *need* it? Like that bulk load of dog food currently taking up most of the shed. Norm could hardly get his bike in and out. He wouldn't have minded, but they didn't actually *have* a dog.

"By the way," said Norm's mum, "did you know you've got your pants on the wrong way round?"

Norm sighed. Of *course* he didn't know he'd got his flipping pants on the wrong way round! Why would anyone *deliberately* do that? All the same Norm was actually quite glad that he *had* put his pants on the wrong way round. They were the ones with *May Contain Nuts* written on the front.

CHAPTER 4

Norm was sitting with his feet on the table, reading a bike magazine when his brothers suddenly burst into the kitchen.

"Dad needs help," said Brian.

"Tell me about it," muttered Norm without even bothering to look up.

"What?" said Brian.

"He's needed help for years if you ask me," said Norm. "If that's all you came here to say, you've said it now, so clear off."

"What you doing?" said Dave.

"Looking at a magazine," said Norm.

"What kind of magazine?" said Dave.

"Bike magazine," said Norm.

"Why?" said Dave.

"Cos I want a new bike."

"Why?"

"Cos I just do, right?"

"That's not a proper answer," said Dave.

"Shut up, Dave, you little freak," said Norm.

"I'm telling!" said Dave.

"Dave?" said Norm.

"Yeah?"

"You've confused me with someone who *gives* a monkey's."

There was a slight pause. Outside, the sound of a

car door slamming was followed by the sound of something being dropped and finally the sound of muffled cursing.

"I *mean* Dad needs help getting the *shopping* in," said Brian.

"No, really?" said Norm.

"Yes, re..." began Brian before stopping. "Oh, I see. You're being sarcastic, aren't you, Norman?"

Norm still didn't bother looking up. Some things were more important than helping to get the shopping in – and reading a bike magazine was one of them.

"Sarcasm is the lowest form of humour, you know," said Brian.

"No, really?" said Norm.

"Yes, I read it in a..." began Brian before stopping again. "You're doing it again aren't you, Norman?"

"Got you, Brian!" laughed Dave.

"Shut up, Dave!" said Brian. "You don't even know what sarcasm means!"

"Yeah I do!" said Dave. "It means..."

"What?" said Brian. "What does it mean, smarty pants?"

"It means... It means," said Dave. "It means you smell, Brian! Doesn't it, Norman?"

But Norm wasn't listening any more. He was reading a text he'd just received.

"Are you going to help, Norman, or am I going to have to unload the car all by myself?" said Norm's dad, standing in the doorway, holding a carrier bag leaking something sticky all over the floor.

"Well, if you wouldn't mind, Dad," said Norm, immediately starting to text back.

"As a matter of fact I'd mind very much," said Norm's dad, his voice getting fractionally higher and a vein on the side of his head visibly starting to throb.

DAD'S ANGRY VEIN

These were telltale signs. Signs that Norm's dad was getting stressed. Signs that everyone else in the family seemed to be able to recognise but which, for some reason, Norm didn't.

"Why can't *they* help?" said Norm, staring venomously in the direction of his younger siblings.

"Because they helped in the supermarket," said Norm's dad. "And what have I told you about putting your feet on the table?"

Norm thought for a moment.

"Er, nothing I don't think, Dad."

"Really?" said Norm's dad, slightly surprised. "In that case, get your feet off the table. And don't let me catch you doing it again."

"What, so if I do it again but you don't actually *catch* me, that's OK then is it?" said Norm.

"No, it is not and don't answer back!" said Norm's dad. "Just get your feet off the table! Now!"

Norm huffed and puffed like he'd just been told to cut the lawn with a pair of nail clippers, but did as he was told and took his feet off the table.

"Ha-ha!" sang Brian.

"Ha-ha!" mimicked Dave.

"Shut up, you little freaks," muttered Norm.

Norm's dad waited for a moment, but Norm still gave no indication that he was going to do anything other than stay exactly where he was.

"So, are you going to help, or what?" said Norm's dad, his voice getting fractionally higher again.

"In a minute," said Norm, finishing off the text and sending it.

Norm's dad took a deep breath and exhaled very slowly before turning and walking back outside.

Norm saw that his brothers were staring at him.

"What?" he said innocently. "Don't look at me! That was all *your* fault!"

"*Our* fault?" said Brian. "How come?"

"Helping at the supermarket?" said Norm. "What did you have to go and do that for?"

Brian looked puzzled.

"We didn't *have* to. We *wanted* to. We get crisps."

"Creeps," muttered Norm.

"Who were you texting?" said Dave.

"None of your flipping business!" said Norm.

"Bet it was a girl," said Brian.

"Well, you're wrong," said Norm. "If you must know, it was Mikey."

"Yeah! Bikey-Mikey!" said Dave.

Norm's dad reappeared carrying another pair of carrier bags.

"Shift," he said to Norm, who was blocking his route to the pantry.

"Can I have some money, Dad?" said Norm, ignoring him.

Norm's dad laughed. "You're serious, aren't you?"

Norm was puzzled. Course he was serious. He needed money to be able to afford the bike of his dreams!

Things didn't get much more serious than *that*!

"Honestly, you've got some nerve, Norman! Sat there doing absolutely nothing!"

"I wasn't doing nothing, I was texting Mikey!" protested Norm.

"Exactly!" said Norm's dad.

"So that's a no then, is it?" said Norm.

"Yes, it's a no!" said Norm's dad. "Now shift!"

"What do you say?" said Norm.

"Now!" yelled Norm's dad.

Norm shifted.

"No need to shout," muttered Norm as his dad disappeared into the pantry.

"What's going on?" said Norm's mum from the doorway, TV remote in hand.

"Nothing, Mum," said Norm. "Can I have some money, please?"

"Money?" said Norm's mum. "What do you want money for?"

Norm pulled a face. "To buy stuff with?"

The room fell suddenly silent. Norm didn't need to turn around to know that his dad had reappeared.

"What have I told you about not answering back, Norman?"

Norm didn't know what to say, or indeed whether to say anything. Surely if he replied, then technically he was answering back, wasn't he?

"Come on, Dave," said Brian, heading outside. "Let's get the rest of the stuff in from the car."

It was the opportunity Norm had been waiting for.

"Wait for me," he said, getting up and following.

CHAPTER 5

"Now can I have some money, Dad?" said Norm from the kitchen doorway, a carrier bag in each hand. "Please?"

Norm's dad looked at Norm, the vein on the side of his head immediately starting to throb again. Not that Norm noticed.

"No, you can't," said Norm's mum, who luckily had noticed.

"But..."

"But what, love?"

"I helped, didn't I?"

"You brought a bit of shopping in! What do you want? A medal?" said Norm's dad.

"No, thanks," said Norm. "Not unless I can melt it down and sell it afterwards."

Norm's dad narrowed his eyes and fixed Norm with a look.

"You can't have any money and that's all there is to it!"

There was a pause. Not just any old pause. One of Norm's *dad's* pauses. And when Norm's dad paused, you *knew* not to argue. Unless you were Norm, of course.

"Why not?" said Norm, genuinely mystified as to how his cunning plan could have backfired.

"Because you *can't*, that's why!" exploded Norm's dad.

"That's not a proper reason," muttered Norm.

"Norman?" glowered Norm's mum. "Can't you see your father's getting stressed?"

Norm – who wouldn't have known his dad was getting stressed if his dad had walked into the room wearing a t-shirt with *I'm getting stressed!* written on it – sighed a world-weary sigh.

"You want a proper reason, Norman?" said Norm's dad.

Norm's mum shot Norm's dad a quick glance.

"Alan, I really don't think now's the..."

"No, no," said Norm's dad holding up a hand. "The boy wants a proper reason? I'll *give* him a proper reason!"

Norm's mum looked out the window. Brian and Dave had got distracted and appeared to be re-enacting a scene from *Star Wars,* using French loaves as light sabres.

"If you must know Norman, things are a bit...tricky at the moment. What with me...not working."

"Tricky?" said Norm.

"Financially," said Norm's mum.

Norm's mum and dad glanced at each other.

"Are we broke or something?" said Norm.

"No, no, love, we're not broke," said Norm's mum, doing her best to raise a reassuring smile. "We're just...having to economise a bit, that's all."

"Economise?" said Norm.

"Yes. We're just being a bit more...careful with our money these days. Just tightening our belts a bit. Why do you think we're buying all this supermarket own-brand stuff?"

Norm hadn't actually noticed before, but now his mum came to mention it, there were rather a lot of own-brand cereal boxes and packets of own-brand biscuits and tins of own-brand beans being unpacked and stacked up on the kitchen worktops. Norm still didn't understand how that affected *him* though. Just because his mum and dad were economising didn't mean *he* had to, did it?

"Because it's cheaper?" said Norm.

"Exactly," said his mum. "Every little helps, as they say!"

Norm's dad took a deep breath. Clearly he hadn't finished yet. "Why do you think we moved in the first place, Norman?"

"Sorry, Dad?" Had Norm heard right? The question had caught him off guard.

"Why do you think we moved in the first place?" repeated Norm's dad.

thought Norm. At *last* he was going to find out the *real* reason his life had been trashed and ruined forever! He was beginning to think they'd done it just to annoy him.

"I don't know, Dad," said Norm.

"We moved here," said Norm's dad, "because we *had* to."

Norm didn't understand.

"Had to?"

"*Had* to," said Norm's dad. "Not because we *wanted* to. Because we *had* to."

"I don't..."

"Couldn't keep up the mortgage repayments."

Norm looked at his mum. Was this true? Norm's mum gave a slight nod and smiled a thin-lipped smile. But Norm's dad still hadn't finished.

"They said if we didn't pay soon they'd repossess the house."

"They?" said Norm.

"The building society."

"We didn't have a choice, Norman," said Norm's mum. "It was either move to a smaller house that we *could* afford, or..." Norm's mum hesitated. "...not have a house at all."

"But I thought..."

"You thought what, Norman?" said Norm's dad.

"Well I mean...you resigned from your job, didn't you, Dad? You left because you wanted to!"

Norm's mum shot Norm's dad a quick glance. Not that Norm noticed.

"And I mean you wouldn't have done that if you'd known things were going to be – you know – tricky or whatever would you? That would be stupid!"

"I ooo **er** ooo" began Norm's dad.

"I don't think your dad thought it would take quite so long to find another job love," said Norm's mum, taking over. "Did you, Alan?"

"What?" said Norm's dad a little distracted. "Er, no, I didn't, no."

Norm was finding it all a bit hard to take in. All this talk of mortgages and houses being repossessed was making his teeth itch.

He didn't even know precisely what his dad's job was. Or even *vaguely* what his dad's job was. Or rather, *had* been. He knew he worked for a company of some sort and that the company made stuff – but he had no idea what kind of stuff – and didn't particularly care either.

"So there you go, Norman," said Norm's dad. "Now you know."

"You won't tell your brothers will you, Norman?" said Norm's mum. "It would only upset them."

Flipping typical, thought Norm. Never mind what *he* thinks. Never mind how *he* feels. As long as his stupid little brothers didn't get upset that, was all that flipping mattered!

"Won't tell us what?" said Brian from the doorway, where he and Dave were standing, nibbling on the ends of their light sabres.

For one brief, delicious moment, Norm contemplated blatantly ignoring his mum and telling his brothers everything. *Deliberately* to upset them. See how *they* flipping well liked it!

"Won't tell us *what*?" said Brian again.

Norm's mum looked pleadingly at Norm. Was he about to spill the beans or not?

"That Santa Claus is actually a woman," said Norm.

Dave promptly burst into tears and ran out of the room.

Norm's dad smiled gratefully at Norm. But just *how* grateful was he? That's what Norm wanted to know.

"Dad?"

"Don't even *think* about it, Norman," said Norm's dad.

CHAPTER 6

They hadn't moved very far. Just from one part of town to another. And it wasn't like it was a big town either. It was actually quite a small town. But that was no consolation to Norm. As far as Norm was concerned they might as well have moved to an entirely different continent.

"Hi, Norm," said Mikey, skidding to a halt on the drive, where Norm was busy putting the finishing touches to a ramp made from planks of wood propped up on bricks.

"Hi," muttered Norm.

"All right?" said Mikey.

"Don't ask," said Norm.

"OK," said Mikey.

"You took your time," said Norm.

"Got lost, didn't I?" said Mikey. "Still not used to you living here."

"Tell me about it," said Norm. "I couldn't even find the flipping toilet last night."

"What happened?"

"Don't ask."

"OK," said Mikey. "Cool ramp by the way."

"No thanks to you," muttered Norm.

Conversation temporarily exhausted, it was time to test the ramp. Norm got on his bike, rode to the end of the drive and turned around. As he'd been the one to do all the work, it seemed only fair that he had first shot.

Pedalling furiously, Norm hit the ramp and flew briefly through the air, before landing, wobbling and jamming on his brakes, just managing to avoid smashing into the garage door.

"That was rubbish!" spat Norm. "Stupid flipping drive!"

"It's not the drive's fault, Norm," said Mikey.

Everything suddenly went very quiet. Even the birds seemed to stop singing for a moment. Norm looked at Mikey.

"What did you say?"

"Er, nothing," said Mikey.

"Of course it's the flipping drive's fault," said Norm. "It's not long enough! You can't get enough speed up!"

Norm glared at Mikey, defying him to disagree. If looks really could kill, Mikey would have dropped dead on the spot.

"It's not *my* fault, Mikey!"

Mikey knew better than to say anything when Norm was in a mood like this. And Norm had been in a mood like this ever since he'd moved.

They'd been friends for as long as they could remember, Norm and Mikey. In fact, they'd been friends even *longer* than they could remember, having first got to know each other at the local parent and toddler group when they were both still in nappies. (There were photos of them kissing each other to prove it.)

They'd lived just round the corner from each other. They'd started school with each other. They'd gone to the same birthday parties as each other. They'd even been on holiday with each other. (There were naked beach photos to prove it.)

So when Norm moved to another part of town, it wasn't only a kick in the dangly bits to Norm, it was a kick in the dangly bits to Mikey, too.

"I know it's rubbish, Norm," said Mikey. "But there's nothing you can do about it now."

"Yeah there is," said Norm. "We could move back to our *old* house."

Mikey laughed as he rode to the end of the drive, ready for his turn.

"I'm serious, Mikey!" said Norm.

"Yeah I know you are," said Mikey. "But let's face it, it's not going to happen, is it?"

Norm thought for a moment.

"Unless..."

"Unless *what*?" said Mikey. "There *is* no unless, Norm! You're here now and you might as well get used to it!"

Mikey was right and Norm knew it. This was real life, not some stupid book where stuff that would never really happen happened. The reality was, another family was living in their old house now and Norm was stuck in a place so small you couldn't swing a cat even if you knocked down all the walls and made one big room.

Norm sighed. Reality could be such a pain sometimes.

Pedalling just a bit more furiously than Norm, Mikey hit the jump and flew just a bit further through the air, landing perfectly and executing an immaculate hundred and eighty degree skid before coming to a halt without ever looking remotely like he was going to smash into the garage door.

"See?" said Norm, knowing full well that Mikey's jump had actually been a bit better than his own.

"Yeah," said Mikey, knowing full well that Norm knew that his jump had been a bit better. Not only that, Mikey was pretty sure Norm *knew* he knew that Norm knew his jump had been a bit better. But he decided not to say anything.

"Why don't you just open the garage door?"

Norm spun round. Brian and Dave had appeared on the drive, eating sweets.

"What?" said Norm, irritably.

"Why don't you open the garage door?" repeated Brian.

"I've got a better idea, Brian," said Norm. "Why don't *you* shut up and go away?"

"Hang on, Norm," said Mikey. "So what you're saying is, if we open the garage door we wouldn't have to stop so suddenly?"

Brian nodded.

"So we could move the jump further up the drive and get a better run at it!"

"Precisely," said Brian.

Norm and Mikey exchanged glances.

"That's actually a really good idea," said Mikey.

"Thanks," said Dave.

Brian glared at his little brother. "What do you mean, *thanks*? It was my idea, not yours!"

"I was being sarcastic," said Dave.

It was then that Norm noticed the sweets.

"What are you eating?"

"Sweets," said
Dave.

"I can see that!"
snapped Norm.
"Where'd you get
the money from?"

"Dad gave it to us," said Brian.

"What for?" said Norm.

"For upsetting Dave," said Brian.

"What?" said Norm.

"Saying that Santa's a woman," said Brian.

Norm looked at his youngest brother. Dave didn't
seem terribly upset now. Then again it couldn't

have been easy, looking upset *and* trying to eat a Curly Wurly sideways.

"Let me get this right," said Norm. "Dad gave you *both* money for sweets because I upset Dave?"

"Pretty much, yeah," said Brian.

"What do you mean, *pretty much*?" said Norm. "Did he or didn't he?"

Brian nodded.

Norm was doing his best to keep calm, but it wasn't easy. Not only did it feel like the whole world was against him, it was beginning to feel like the rest of the solar system was too.

"*That* is !" hissed Norm.

Sensing it was probably time to leave, Brian grabbed Dave by the arm and began marching him towards the house. Mikey, meanwhile, had already opened the garage door and shifted the ramp.

"Try that, Norm," he said.

Norm cycled to the end of the drive, turned around and started pedalling as fast as he could. But by now Norm was barely in control of his emotions, let alone his bike, and the extra run-up made no noticeable difference. If anything, he flew into the air even more briefly than before.

"Stupid flipping bike!" yelled Norm.

"So it's the bike now, is it?" said Mikey.

"Well it's not *my* fault!" said Norm.

"Wanna swap?" suggested Mikey, whose bike was actually a bit better than Norm's.

"What?"

"Wanna swap bikes?"

"Don't mind," shrugged Norm nonchalantly. "If you want."

Norm and Mikey swapped bikes. Mikey rode to the end of the drive, turned round and prepared to try again. Pedalling even more furiously than before, he hit the ramp and shot into the air.

"Whoa!!" yelled Mikey, as he disappeared into the gloom of the garage.

There was the briefest of pauses, followed immediately by a loud crashing noise.

"Oops," said Norm.

"Ow," groaned Mikey.

"Aaaaaaaand cut!" said a voice from the other side of the fence.

Norm turned around. A girl he'd never seen before was standing in next-door's garden, looking at her phone and laughing hysterically.

"Brilliant," she said. "That's the funniest thing I've ever seen!"

"Did you just film that?" said Norm.

"Yeah, why?" said the girl. "You got a problem with that?"

"Er, yeah, I have, actually!"

Norm wasn't sure exactly what his problem was, but he knew that he had one. It didn't matter though, because at that moment his dad suddenly appeared.

"

What was that?"

"That what, Dad?" said Norm innocently.

"That smashing sound?"

"What smashing sound, Dad?" said Norm. "I didn't hear anything."

"You'd better not have broken anything, Norman!" said Norm's dad, heading inside the garage.

The girl next door was looking at Norm and smirking.

"What are you looking at?" said Norm.

"Is that really your name?" said the girl. "*Norman*?"

"What the...?" exploded Norm's dad.

"Oh, *that* smashing sound, Dad!" said Norm. "You should've said!"

CHAPTER 7

Norm's dad stood, open-mouthed, surveying the scene. Shards of shattered porcelain made random patterns on the garage floor. Flattened cardboard boxes lay scattered like giant placemats. Somewhere in the middle sat a slightly dazed-looking Mikey.

"Are you all right, Mikey?"

"Yeah, I think so, thanks, Mr B," said Mikey, getting up and brushing away what appeared to be a teacup handle from the front of his jeans.

"Never mind *him*!" said Norm, indignantly. "What about my flipping bike?"

"Never mind your bike, Norman!" said Norm's dad. "Look what you've done! That's your mum's tea set that is! Or at least it *was*, anyway!"

Norm couldn't believe what he was hearing. "Me?" he squeaked. "It wasn't *me* who crashed, Dad, it was Mikey!" By now, Norm had picked up his bike and was inspecting it for damage.

"Aw, flip!"

"What is it?" said Mikey.

"The front forks are all bent!"

"Sorry, Norm," said Mikey, sheepishly.

"I'll have to get new ones!"

"Well, *I'm* not paying for them!" said Norm's dad. "It's your own fault!"

Norm looked at his dad.

"Are you talking to *me*, Dad?"

"Who do you *think* I'm talking to?"

"I already told you! It wasn't *me* riding the bike, it was Mikey!"

"Don't blame Mikey, Norman!"

"Didn't you hear him?" said Norm. "He just said sorry!"

"Leave Mikey out of this, Norman! Whose idea was it in the first place?"

Norm didn't answer immediately. Instead, determined to enjoy the moment, he allowed himself a slight smile of satisfaction.

"Well?" said Norm's dad.

"Brian's," said Norm.

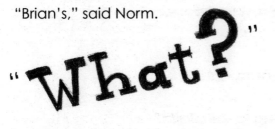

"It was Brian's idea," said Norm. "He said we

should open the garage door so we could move the ramp and get a better run-up."

"Did he now?" said Norm's dad.

"He certainly did, Dad," said Norm, smugly.

"And if Brian told you to jump off a cliff you'd do that as well, would you?"

"What?"

"You should've known better, Norman! You're twelve years old for goodness sake!"

"Nearly thirteen, actually," said Norm, like that was somehow going to make things better.

"Look at it," said Norm's dad.

Norm looked at it. "It's just a few old cups and saucers," he said. "What's the big deal?"

 " said Norm's dad.

Norm shrugged. He genuinely couldn't see what all the fuss was about. If the tea set really *was* that special how come it hadn't been unpacked yet? And if his mum really *was* that bothered she could just buy another one from one of the shopping channels, couldn't she?

"That belonged to your grandma that did, Norman," said Norm's dad, wistfully. "It's of great sentimental value. Or at least it *was* of great sentimental value."

"Stupid place to put it," muttered Norm.

"Correction," said Norm's dad. "Perfectly *sensible* place to put it. *Stupid* place to ride your bike!"

"Dad?"

"What?"

"It *wasn't* me! It's not my fault!"

"I dread to think what your grandpa's going to say!"

"I'd better be off then," said Mikey, getting back on his own bike, apparently none the worse for wear.

"Wait for me, Mikey," said Norm, following behind.

"Where do you think *you're* going?" said Norm's dad.

"Biking?" said Norm.

"No way, Norman," said Norm's dad. "First things first – you clear up this mess. And when you've done that you can go and apologise to your mother."

"But..."

"No buts, Norman."

"I'll do it later, Dad! I promise!"

"You will *not* do it later, Norman, you'll do it *now!*"

Norm sighed and watched as Mikey disappeared down the street. How he wished *he* could have disappeared as well. He didn't care where to. As long as it was away from his tight-fisted parents and his stupid little brothers. And his stupid, *stupid* little house!

CHAPTER 8

It took Norm the best part of an hour to clear up the mess in the garage, and less than ten seconds to find his mum. He knew exactly where she'd be. And he was right.

"I'm afraid there's been a bit of an accident, Mum," said Norm, slumping down on the sofa.

"That's nice, love," said Norm's mum absentmindedly, eyes fixed firmly on the TV, where a woman with a fake tan and an even more fake smile was doing her best to sound enthusiastic about cutlery.

It occurred to Norm that he could say just about anything he liked right now and get away with it. His mum wasn't listening.

"I've got something to tell you, Mum."

There was no reply from Norm's mum.

"I'm not really your son."

Norm paused for maximum dramatic effect.

"You adopted me when I was a baby."

There was no indication that Norm's mum was paying any attention to a word Norm was saying. Norm wondered how far he could push it.

"I was raised by zebras in the Belgian rainforest before being discovered by hunters and taken to a nearby town."

There was *still* no reaction from Norm's mum. Result, thought Norm. All he had to do was tell his dad he'd apologised and hope he didn't bother to check.

"I must leave now," said Norm, getting up. "It is time for me to return. My people await me. Farewell my so-called mother."

Norm was halfway to the door before his mum eventually spoke.

"There's no rainforest in Belgium, love."

Norm stopped dead in his tracks.
"What, Mum?"

"There's no rainforest in Belgium."

"Er, not any more there isn't," said Norm. "It's all been destroyed."

"There are no zebras, either."

"Extinct."

"What was that about an accident?"

Flip, thought Norm. So his mum obviously *had* been listening after all. Was that what they called multi-tasking?

"It wasn't my fault," said Norm.

"What wasn't?"

Norm hesitated.

"Smashing the tea set."

"My eighteen-piece antique tea set?" said Norm's mum.

"More like a *hundred* and eighteen pieces now I'm afraid, Mum."

"Don't worry about it."

"Pardon?" said Norm.

"I really don't want to talk about it at the moment, Norman," said Norm's mum, zapping to the next shopping channel, where a man who made the woman selling cutlery seem pale and sickly by comparison was demonstrating some kind of drill.

This wasn't what Norm had been expecting at all. He'd been expecting his mum to be really upset. Worse than that he'd been expecting some kind of punishment – like being banned off the computer or Xbox.

"It was a stupid thing to do," said Norm. "We should never have listened to Brian."

"Norman?"

"Yes, Mum?"

Soo stupid

"I said I don't want to talk about it at the moment."

Norm hated it when other people didn't want to talk about stuff and he did, conveniently forgetting that it was normally the other way round. Normally it was Norm who didn't want to talk about stuff and other people who did. Other people could be so flipping annoying, thought Norm.

"When do you think you *will* want to talk about it, Mum?" said Norm, who needed to know what he was going to be banned from doing and for how long. Not knowing was a form of punishment in itself.

Norm's mum sighed. "What do you want me to say, Norman? Ten minutes? An hour-and-a-half? I don't know when I'll want to talk about it! If I even *think* about talking about it I'm going to get upset. And there's been enough upset lately." Sensing that she might have said too much, Norm's mum shot Norman a quick glance.

"What do you mean, Mum?"

"Nothing, love!" said Norm's mum breezily, zapping channels again. "Ooh, look! Beach towels!"

Norm knew that his mum was trying to change the subject.

To the best of his knowledge they had more than enough beach towels already. Besides, if what his dad had told him earlier was true, there wouldn't be much need for beach towels in the future. In fact if what his dad had told him earlier was true, they'd be lucky to ever have another holiday again, let alone to anywhere with a beach.

"Do you mean the money thing, Mum?"

Norm's mum glanced at Norman again, but didn't say anything. She didn't need to.

"You do, don't you?"

Norm's mum muted the sound on the TV – a sure-fire sign that things were about to get serious, thought Norm. If an unexploded bomb from World War Two had been discovered buried in the garden his mum *might* have turned the volume down a bit – but actual muting was virtually unheard of.

"Your dad'll go mad if he knows I've told you, love."

Told me what? thought Norm.

"He doesn't want anyone to know."

Know what? thought Norm.

"You won't say anything will you, Norman?"

Not if you don't flipping well hurry up and tell me I won't, thought Norm.

"Well, Norman?"

"Mum's the word, Mum," said Norm.

Norm's mum looked around to make sure they were still alone.

"He didn't resign."

"What?" said Norm.

"Your dad. He didn't resign from his job. He was made redundant."

"What do you mean, Mum?"

"They got rid of him."

"Why?" said Norm.

"I don't know, love. Something about cutbacks. He was a bit vague when I asked him."

They sat in silence for several seconds while Norm tried to make sense of things. So his dad had been telling porkies, had he? But why? It wasn't that big a deal, was it? What difference did it make, resigning or being made redundant? Like simultaneous equations and poetry, adults were a complete mystery to Norm. It would have been so much simpler if he really *had* been raised by zebras in the Belgian rainforest.

"Have I interrupted something?" said Norm's dad from the doorway.

"What makes you think that?" said Norm's mum,

wondering how long he'd been there.

"The TV's on mute."

"So it is!" said Norm's mum doing her best to sound surprised. "How did that happen, Norman?"

But Norm wasn't paying attention. He was too busy staring at his dad.

"What's up?" said Norm's dad.

"Uh? What?" said Norm.

"Why are you looking at me like that?"

But before Norm could think of a reply, the TV was suddenly un-muted.

"Ooh, look!" said Norm's mum breezily. "Cushion covers!"

CHAPTER 9

As it happened, Norm's grandpa could hardly have cared less about the tea set when Norm told him about it later that day.

"Ach, don't worry about it," he said, carrying on digging his allotment. "Never liked it much anyway."

"What?" said Norm. "Seriously, Grandpa?"

"Seriously," said Grandpa. "I was going to give it to a charity shop but your mum wanted to keep it. It's no big deal."

"That's exactly what I said!" shrieked Norm. "But Dad reckoned it was like, sentimental or something!"

"Talking out his backside as usual then, wasn't he?" said Grandpa.

Norm grinned.

"It's true," said Grandpa. "And I'll tell you something else for nothing."

"What?" said Norm.

"I never liked your dad much, either."

Norm burst out laughing.

"I'm not joking, Norman! I tried to put your mother off marrying him but she wouldn't listen. Kids never do."

"Pardon?" said Norm.

"Very funny," said Grandpa drily. "Now do something useful and fetch me that wheelbarrow."

Norm went to fetch the wheelbarrow. His grandpa really did come out with the most outrageous things sometimes. The sort of things most people *thought* but never actually *said* out loud. Grandpa was the complete opposite. He just blurted out whatever was on his mind. He didn't seem to care who he offended. But for some reason, with Grandpa it was very hard to actually *be* offended. It was even harder not to like him.

"I'm so relieved, Grandpa," said Norm, wheeling back the wheelbarrow.

"About what?" said Grandpa.

"The tea set?" said Norm. "I thought you were going to go ballistic!"

"Why would I go ballistic?" said Grandpa. "It's just stuff at the end of the day, Norman. I've got way too much stuff already. I'm trying to get *rid* of stuff! What do I want more stuff for? I'm nearly dead."

"No, you're not, Grandpa!" laughed Norm. "You're nowhere near dead yet!"

"As long as I can still come down here, I'll be happy," said Grandpa. "As long as I can still grow my runner beans and my lettuces and my courgettes. That's all *I'm* bothered about."

"Nothing else?" said Norm.

Grandpa stopped digging and leaned on his spade. "Such as?"

"Your grandchildren?" suggested Norm, hopefully.

"Pain in the backside, grandchildren. Always scrounging sweets and wanting you to play with them."

"You know you don't mean it, Grandpa," said Norm.

"I mean every word. And I'll tell you something else for nothing."

"What?" said Norm.

"You're the biggest pain of the lot."

Grandpa's eyes crinkled ever so slightly in the corners. It was the closest he ever came to smiling.

"Love you too, Grandpa," grinned Norm.

"And you can pack *that* in as well," said Grandpa. "All that lovey-dovey-touchy-feely-kissy-wissy stuff. Next thing you'll be wanting to give me a hug!"

Norm laughed.

"I'm serious!" said Grandpa. "People never used to hug each other or say they loved each other every two minutes when I was growing up! In those days a kick up the backside was considered a sign of affection. Not like now – everyone going round giving each other high fives or whatever you call them. What's wrong with a good firm handshake? That's what I'd like to know!"

In the distance a church bell chimed three times.

"That time already?" said Grandpa, fishing in his pocket and producing a pound coin. "Nip along to the shops and get me a packet of biscuits would you, Norman?"

"What kind of biscuits, Grandpa?"

"Proper biscuits."

"Proper biscuits?" said Norm.

"Something I can dunk in my tea," said Grandpa. "Preferably digestives. None of your bourbon or custard cream nonsense or those ones with the hole in the middle."

"Jammie Dodgers?" said Norm.

"Yeah, those," said Grandpa.

"Aw, they're the *best*, Grandpa!"

"You think?"

"I *know*!"

"Well you're wrong," said Grandpa giving the pound coin to Norm. "Now hurry up. I'm growing a beard here."

"What's it worth?" said Norm.

"What? You mean in euros?" said Grandpa.

"I meant what's it worth to go to the shops and buy you the biscuits," said Norm.

Grandpa looked at Norm. "You a bit hard up, are you?"

"You could say that, yeah," said Norm.

"You saving up for something?"

Norm nodded. "New bike."

"A new bike, eh?" said Grandpa stroking his chin. "In that case you'd better keep the change."

Norm didn't know exactly how much a packet of digestives would cost, but he was pretty sure there wouldn't be much change from a pound. He tried to look grateful, but obviously not hard enough.

"What's the matter?" said Grandpa.

"Nothing," said Norm.

Grandpa sighed.

Here we go, thought Norm. A lecture about how when Grandpa was his age a pound was a lot of money and how you could buy a car for five quid and a house for less than a hundred and blah blah blah. Well so flipping what? That was like, back in the 70s or something. That wasn't just history – that was *ancient* history!

But Norm couldn't have been more wrong. Instead of a lecture, Grandpa put his hand back in his pocket and pulled out a ten-pound note.

Norm's eyes widened.

"Come to daddy," he whispered.

"Pardon?" said Grandpa.

"Er, I mean thanks very much, Grandpa!" said Norm, taking the money. "Gimme fi... I mean...gimme a good firm handshake!"

They shook hands.

"This is just between you and me, right?" said Grandpa. "Don't tell your brothers now, will you?"

"Course not, Grandpa!" said Norm, heading down the path.

Norm stopped and thought for a second.

"Er, Grandpa?"

"What is it?"

"Do I still get to keep the change from the pound?"

Norm didn't hang around long enough for an answer, but a second later a courgette whizzed past him, narrowly missing his left ear.

"I'll take that as a no, then," laughed Norm.

CHAPTER 10

There was only one thing Norm wanted more than a new bike and that was to be an only child again. To return to those distant, carefree days when the world seemed to revolve around him and him alone. When the slightest cough would have his mum rushing for medical books to check for signs of possible fatal diseases. When performing basic farmyard impressions was a sure-fire sign of genius. When breaking wind at the dinner table was considered funny, not gross.

But those days were long gone. These days Brian and Dave were the centre of the universe. These days Norm could walk through the door on crutches, wearing a pink tutu and his parents wouldn't bat an eyelid.

Not that Norm resented his little brothers *all* the time. Sure there were some days he would have happily sold them on eBay – but equally there were other days when Norm just about tolerated Brian and Dave. There was even the odd day when, for some inexplicable reason, they very nearly got on with each other. This, however, didn't look like it was going to be one of those days.

"Oh, come on, Dave, I was joking!" said Norm. "Santa's not *really* a woman!"

It was the next morning and Dave still hadn't forgiven Norm. Relations had gradually improved to the point where they were now able to sit in the same room together, but Dave could hold a grudge pretty much as long as he wanted to, if he put his mind to it.

"Promise?"

Norm bit his tongue. He knew he had to be careful what he said here if he didn't want a row from his parents about 'spoiling it for his brothers'. Spoiling it? His flipping brothers went and flipping spoilt it by being born in the flipping first place!

"Promise," said Norm.

"Was that really what you were talking about?"

"What do you mean?" said Norm.

"I mean when me and Brian walked in the room yesterday," said Dave. "You weren't really talking about Santa were you? You were talking about something else. I could tell."

Norm looked at Dave. Not only could he be unbelievably stubborn, he could be surprisingly perceptive sometimes for a seven-year-old.

"What's it to you?"
shrugged Norm.

"Just wondering,"
said Dave.

"Anyway, what if Santa
is a woman?" said Norm,
keen to change the subject. "What's wrong with
that?"

"So he does exist then?" Dave shot back, quick as
a flash.

"Or *she*," said Norm, beginning to wish he'd
changed the subject to a *different* subject.

Luckily for Norm, Brian saved him the bother by
walking into the room at that moment.

"Ugh! What the heck's *that*?" said Norm.

"It's Brian," said Dave.

"I mean what the heck's that *next* to Brian?"
said Norm.

Dave craned his neck to have a look. Something small, fat and hairy was sat by Brian's feet, dribbling on the carpet.

"I'm not sure," said Dave. "I think it might be a dog."

"A dog?" snorted Norm derisively. "Looks more like a mop without the handle!"

"Don't listen to him, Simon Cowell!" said Brian, bending down and giving whatever it was a pat on the back.

"Simon Cowell?" said Norm in disbelief.

"He's *my* dog," said Brian. "I'll call him what I like!"

"What do you mean, *your* dog?"

"I found him."

"Where?"

"In the street."

"That doesn't mean you can keep it!" said Norm.

"Why not?" said Brian.

"What do you mean, *why not*?" said Norm, getting more and more exasperated. "You can't just keep everything you find!"

"Why not?" said Brian.

"Don't just keep saying 'why not', Brian!"

"Why not?" said Brian.

Norm took a deep breath. He didn't particularly *want* to get in an argument with Brian. It was very hard not to sometimes, though.

"How do you know it's even lost in the first place?" said Norm.

"I don't," said Brian.

"Well something has to be *lost* before you can *find* it!" said Norm.

"So?" said Brian.

"So you can't keep it can you?" said Norm. Norm was feeling quite pleased with himself. Brian had wanted a reason and now he'd got one.

"Why not?" said Brian.

"Because you flipping well can't, that's why!" yelled Norm, finally losing what little patience he'd had to begin with. "What are you? Stupid or something?"

"Yeah, Brian," taunted Dave. "What are you? Stupid or something?"

"Shut up, Dave!" said Brian. "And anyway I *am* going to keep it and you can't stop me so there!"

Norm looked at the dog, which by now had started to lick itself in places Norm had previously thought were impossible to lick. Not that Norm had spent much time thinking about it.

"OK, just *suppose* you keep it," said Norm.

"*Him* – not *it*," said Brian defiantly. "And I *am* going to."

"Whatever," said Norm. "Have you any idea how much it costs to keep a dog?"

Brian shrugged. "Doesn't matter," he said. "We've got tons of dog food already."

Norm couldn't argue with *that* – much as he would have liked to. Thanks to his mum's escalating shopping channel habit they had enough dog food in the shed to feed a whole herd of dogs – or whatever the proper word for a bunch of dogs was.

"It's not just food," said Norm. "There's other stuff too."

Brian shrugged again. "I'll use my own money."

"What money?" said Norm. "You haven't *got* any money, Brian!"

"Yeah I have," said Brian. "Grandpa gave me ten pounds."

"What?" said Norm.

The room suddenly went very quiet. Even the dog stopped what it was doing and looked up expectantly.

"Grandpa gave you some money?" said Norm.

Brian nodded.

"When?" said Norm, as calmly as possible.

"Yesterday," said Brian.

"Me too," chirped Dave. "Grandpa said not to tell you, though."

Brian and Dave looked at each other.

said Dave.

The room suddenly went even quieter than the last time. But not for long.

"That is so un-flipping-fair!" bellowed Norm, jumping to his feet.

"It's not our fault!" protested Brian.

"Course it's your flipping fault!" Norm yelled.

Norm stared at Brian, like a python eyeing up its prey.

"Give it to me," he said.

"What?" said Brian.

"The money!" said Norm. "Give it to me! Both of you! Now!"

"Why should we?" said Dave.

"Why should you?" said Norm. "Why *shouldn't* you?"

The dog barked.

"And you can shut up!" spat Norm.

"Don't listen to him, Simon Cowell," said Brian, kneeling down and giving the dog another pat.

It was then that Norm noticed the metal tag attached to the dog's collar. A metal tag which would most likely have a phone number engraved on it. Someone somewhere would no doubt be very grateful to receive a call. But exactly *how* grateful? wondered Norm. Everything had its price. What was the going rate for a small, fat, hairy, dribbling mop?

As if reading Norm's mind, the dog leapt up and started licking Brian full in the face.

"Oh, that is *so* disgusting!" said Norm.

"He's just licking my face," said Brian.

"Yeah – but you didn't see what it was licking a minute ago," said Norm.

CHAPTER 11

Norm punched the numbers into his mobile and waited. Someone picked up after a couple of rings.

"Hello?" said a bored-sounding voice.

"Hello," said Norm quietly, so that no one else could hear. "I've found your dog."

"What? You mean alive?" said the voice.

"Er, yeah," said Norm, slightly puzzled.

"I see," said the voice.

It wasn't quite the reaction Norm had been expecting when he'd snuck into his parents' room to make the call. He'd assumed that whoever answered might at least sound vaguely happy to learn that their beloved four-legged friend had been discovered safe and sound and not as flat as a Frisbee at the side of a road somewhere.

"How do you know it's mine?"

"Er, well, it's got one of those tag things round its neck?" said Norm. "That's how I got this number."

"What does it look like?"

Norm was getting confused. "Er, well, it's like a small round disc thing? Like a coin?"

"I meant what does the *dog* look like?" said the voice. "I've got a few."

"Oh, right!" said Norm.

Norm looked at the dog, which – clearly exhausted from having to climb an entire flight of stairs – had collapsed onto the floor, panting and wheezing, like a footballer giving a post-match interview. What should he say? Should he pretend that he thought the dog was really cute in the hope that he might get a bigger reward? Or should he just be honest?

"It looks like a fat, dribbling mop," said Norm. "No offence."

"None taken," said the voice. "That'll be Limahl."

"Limahl?" said Norm.

The dog pricked up its ears at the mention of its proper name.

"Singer in a band called Kajagoogoo," said

the voice. "Briefly big in the mid-eighties. Ask your dad."

"Right."

"Put him on the line."

Norm pulled a face. "Who? My dad?"

"No – Limahl," said the voice.

If it was actually possible for the conversation to get any weirder, it just had.

"It's for you," said Norm, holding the phone towards the dog.

The dog looked at Norm. It clearly had no intention of ever moving again if it could possibly help it. Norm sighed and stood up.

"Trying to connect you," said Norm to the voice on the other end of the line.

"You'll need to hold the phone," said the voice.

Norman sighed again. He'd kind of figured that bit out for himself. Kneeling down next to the dog, he put the phone against one of its decidedly mangy-looking ears. A moment or two later the dog began yapping excitedly and wagging its sorry excuse for a tail.

Yap! Yap! Yap! Yap! Yap! Yap!

"What the…?" said Norm's mum, from the doorway.

Norm turned round. His mum looked gobsmacked. Whether this was from finding a dog in her bedroom, or from finding a dog on the *phone* in her bedroom, was hard to tell.

"Get it out, Norman!"

"In a minute, Mum."

"Never mind in a minute, Norman!" yelled

Norm's mum. "Get it out *now!*"

As it happened, Norm didn't have to go to the bother of getting the dog out himself. Possibly sensing that it had outstayed its welcome, the dog had already struggled to its feet and was waddling towards the stairs.

Norm wiped the phone on his sleeve before putting it back to his own ear.

"Hello?" he said. "Are you still there?"

"Where else would I be?" said the voice on the line.

"Who are you talking to?" said Norm's mum.

Deciding it might not be a great idea to tell his mum he was talking to a complete stranger, Norm tried to bluff it out instead.

"Er, Mikey, Mum."

"How did you know my name's Mikey?" said the voice.

"I didn't," said Norm.

"Because it's not."

"What?" said Norm.

"It's Trevor."

"Right," said Norm.

Norm wondered how he was going to be able to ask for money with his mum standing there listening to every word he was saying.

"Do you, er...want it back then?"

"Who? Limahl?" said Trevor.

"Yeah," said Norm.

"Not particularly," said Trevor.

"What?" said Norm.

"You can keep it if you want."

Norm's plan was rapidly going pear-shaped. He wanted money – not some stupid, flea-bitten dog.

"Er, no, you're all right thanks," said Norm.

"I'll pay you," said Trevow.

"What?" said Norm. *"You'll* pay *me?"*

"Yeah."

"How much?" said Norm.

There was a pause on the other end of the line. Trevor was obviously mulling things over.

"A pound?" he said at last.

"A pound?" said Norm. "Is that all?"

Norm couldn't believe it. Surely a dog was worth more than a pound wasn't it? Even a rubbish one.

"You drive a hard bargain," said Trevor. "One pound fifty. My final offer."

"You're joking!" said Norm. "One pound fifty?"

"For what?" said Norm's mum, starting to get suspicious. "Give me that phone, Norman!"

"Er, gotta go, Trev... I mean, Mikey. See you later," said Norm, putting the phone down quickly.

"Where's Simon Cowell?" said Brian from the doorway.

"Simon Cowell?" said Norm's mum.

"He means the dog," said Norm.

"I found him," said Brian.

"Its real name's Limahl," said Norm.

"Limahl?" said Norm's mum.

"Singer in a band called Kaja—"

"—googoo, yes I know that, Norman! Now can someone please tell me what's going—"

Norm's mum stopped abruptly, as if she ran on electricity and someone had suddenly pulled the plug out.

"Phwoar!" she said, wrinkling her nose and wafting a hand in front of her face.

"Phwoar!" said Brian, doing exactly the same.

"What?" said Dave. "I can't smell anything."

Norm swivelled round to see his youngest brother. Where had *he* appeared from? More importantly, why was there a trail of brown sticky footprints leading from the landing to where he now stood in the middle of the room?

"My rug!" wailed Norm's mum.

"There's dog mess on my rug!"

"Norman!" yelled Norm's dad from the bottom of the stairs.

"What?" yelled Norm. "It's not *my* fault!"

"That's from IKEA that is!" said Norm's mum, like it was somehow OK to squidge dog mess into a rug that wasn't.

CHAPTER 12

It wasn't so much the fact that he got the blame for Limahl/Simon Cowell doing a massive dump in the middle of the hall that bothered Norm. He knew he'd get the blame eventually. What *bothered* Norm was the fact that he was *automatically* blamed. Like it couldn't *possibly* have been anyone else's fault. Like it had never, for a single nanosecond, crossed his dad's mind that maybe – just *maybe* – one of his brothers might have had something to do with it.

"Well?" said Norm's dad. "How do you explain *that*, Norman?"

"Easy, Dad," said Norm, slaloming down the stairs between brown footprints. "Food goes in one end and—"

"You know perfectly well what I mean, Norman!"

Norm shrugged. "Well it wasn't *me*, Dad!"

"I should hope not!" said Norm's dad. "Peeing in my wardrobe was bad enough!"

"*Nearly* peeing in your wardrobe," corrected Norm.

But Norm's dad wasn't listening. The vein on the side of his head was beginning to throb. Not that Norm noticed.

"Have you *any* idea how hard that's going to be to clean up?"

"Why are you asking *me*, Dad?" said Norm. "Ask Brian!"

Norm's dad pulled a face. "Why would I ask Brian?"

"Because it was *Brian* who found it in the first place!"

"What are you talking about, Norman?"

"The dog! Brian found it. He wants to keep it. It's called Limahl, but Brian wants to call it Simon Cowell."

Norm didn't know why he was even bothering to explain. There could be CCTV footage of Brian walking through the door with the dog and it wouldn't make the slightest bit of difference now. His dad had made his mind up. Norm was guilty – and the sooner he admitted it and faced up to whatever punishment was coming his way the better.

Which reminded Norm. He still hadn't been punished for destroying his mum's tea set the day before. Or rather, he still hadn't been punished for *Mikey* destroying his mum's tea set the day before. Unless of course his dad thought Norm had already been punished? Norm certainly wasn't going to say anything, just in case.

"Look at it!" said Norm's dad staring intently at the carpet.

Norm looked at it. For a relatively small dog, Limahl/Simon Cowell had certainly produced an eye-wateringly large dump.

"What do you want me to say, Dad?"

"How about SORRY , Norman?"

"But..."

"We're probably going to have to get the carpets professionally cleaned. And that's the *last* thing we need right now!"

"Yeah, I wonder why *that* is," muttered Norm under his breath.

Norm knew he shouldn't have said it as soon as he said it. Not only that, Norm's dad *knew* that Norm knew that he shouldn't have said it as soon as he said it.

"What was that, Norman?"

"Er, I was just wondering why that's the last thing we need right now," said Norm.

Norm's dad sighed wearily.

"Because getting the carpets cleaned will cost *money*, Norman. And we don't *have* a lot of money at the moment. I thought we talked about this yesterday?"

"Forgot," said Norm.

Norm's dad looked at Norm. "You forgot?"

Norm nodded.

"You're getting a bit forgetful in your old age aren't you, Norman?"

Norm shrugged.

"First you 'forget' that we moved house three months ago," said Norm's dad, making speech marks in the air with his fingers. "Then you 'forget' a conversation we had just yesterday, explaining precisely *why* we moved house three months ago."

"I know," grinned Norm. "What am I like?"

"Fish oil," said Norm's dad.

Norm pulled a face. This would have been a pretty random thing for Grandpa to suddenly blurt out, never mind his dad!

"Good for your memory."

"What is?" said Norm.

"Fish oil," said Norm's dad.

"Right," said Norm.

"I take it myself," said Norm's dad.

"When you remember to," said Norm.

"Pardon?"

"It was a joke, Dad."

"This is no laughing matter, Norman!" said Norm's dad. "This is very serious!"

"Yeah, I know," said Norm. "Mum told me."

Once again Norm knew he shouldn't have said it as soon as he said it. Not only that but once again Norm's dad *knew* that Norm knew that he shouldn't have said it as soon as he said it.

They looked at each other for a moment. The atmosphere had suddenly changed. Dog poo was no longer number one on the agenda. Dog poo was number two.

"What's she told you?" said Norm's dad.

"About what, Dad?"

"Don't play dumb, Norman. What's Mum told you?"

Like a rabbit caught in the beams of a car's headlights, Norm felt gripped by an almost numbing sense of indecisiveness. He knew that his dad had been made redundant, but he also knew that he wasn't *meant* to know. What was he supposed to say? The last thing Norm wanted was to get his mum into trouble. Well, strictly speaking that was the *second* last thing he wanted. The actual *last* thing Norm wanted was to get *himself* into trouble. Or at least more trouble than he was in already!

"Sorry, Norman, I shouldn't have done that."

"What?" said Norman.

"I shouldn't have put you in that position. It was very unfair of me. I'm sorry."

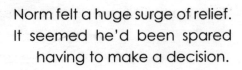

Norm felt a huge surge of relief. It seemed he'd been spared having to make a decision.

"It's OK, Dad."

"I wish things weren't so difficult, son."

Tell me about it, thought Norm.

"It'll get better," said Norm's dad, trying to smile. "Trust me."

Norm suddenly felt really bad. Whatever his dad had been going through couldn't have been easy. He obviously had his reasons for not wanting Norm to find out that he'd been made redundant. If only Norm knew what those reasons were.

"I'll give you five pounds," said Norm's dad, fixing Norman with a steely stare.

"What?" said Norm.

"Five pounds if you tell me everything Mum told you."

Norm suddenly felt like a rabbit again – but not a rabbit in the beam of a car's headlights. A rabbit that had thought it was being taken out of its hutch for a stroke, but then found itself chucked in a casserole dish with only an onion and a couple of potatoes for company.

"Erm…" said Norm.

Norm's dad laughed. "I'm kidding!"

Norm tried to laugh too, but nothing came out.

"*There* you are, Simon Cowell!" yelled Brian from the top of the stairs. "I've been looking everywhere for you!"

Norm and his dad turned round to see the dog waddling out of the kitchen. Was it Norm's imagination, or was it smiling? No, thought Norm. That was impossible. Dogs couldn't smile, could they?

"Get that thing out of here!" thundered Norm's dad.

"No, Dad! Pleeeeeeease!" wailed Brian.

Norm's dad sniffed and headed for the kitchen, wafting a hand in front of his face.

Norm looked at the dog.
"Not again, surely?"
said Norm.

The dog looked at Norm. *You got a problem with that?* it seemed to say.

Sensing that he'd have a very big problem if he hung around much longer, Norm opened the front door and snuck out. The dog – obviously not as stupid as it looked – followed behind.

"Come back, Simon Cowell!" wailed Brian.

"Norman!" yelled Norm's dad from the kitchen.

But it was too late. Both dog and Norm had left the building.

CHAPTER 13

Norm's first thought on escaping from the house was to get on his bike and ride. His second thought was to wonder where to ride his bike *to*. Not that he had to wonder very long. Mikey's was the obvious choice of destination. Not only was Mikey Norm's best friend, he didn't have annoying parents, even more annoying little brothers, or pets named after random eighties pop stars. Best of all though, the drive at Mikey's house was so big it was practically visible from space. No need to open the garage door to get a decent run-up there.

The only problem was that it took more time to actually *get* to Mikey's since they'd moved. Not that that was much of a problem for someone as crazy about biking as Norm. Norm practically lived and breathed biking. To Norm, biking was no ordinary fad or craze – it was a way of life.

So actually, in a weird kind of way – and not that Norm would have *ever* admitted it – Norm's parents had done Norm a favour by moving house. Riding to Mikey's was now more fun than it ever used to be. Instead of just living round the corner, Mikey now lived round *lots* of corners, with a couple of hills and a set of steps at the back of the shopping precinct thrown in for good measure. Instead of only taking *one* song on Norman's iPod like it used to, the journey could now take four or five songs, depending on the length of song and how much welly Norm was giving it.

Mikey was doing a wheelie when Norm eventually arrived. In fact, rather annoyingly as far as Norm was concerned, Mikey was doing an extremely *good* wheelie when Norm eventually arrived. It was just so flipping unfair, thought Norm. It was him who'd got Mikey into biking in the first flipping place. Mikey had been more into computer games and books and playing his stupid drums. If it hadn't been for Norm, Mikey probably wouldn't have even *had* a bike!

Of course it wasn't Mikey's fault he turned out to be a naturally gifted biker and just that little bit better than Norm. But then it wasn't Mikey's fault that he was just that little bit better than Norm at virtually everything. It wasn't Mikey's fault he always seemed to do just that little bit better at school than Norm without ever having to work very hard. He didn't do it on purpose. He didn't *try* to be better. He just *was*.

"All right, Norm?" said Mikey as Norm skidded to a halt.

"All right," said Norm.

"Forks OK then, are they?"

"What?" said Norm.

"Your front forks?" said Mikey looking at Norm's bike. "I thought they were all bent."

"Oh right, yeah," said Norm. "They're er...not as bad as I thought they were. Just a bit scratched, that's all."

"That's good then," said Mikey.

"Yeah," said Norm.

"Wasn't expecting to see you today," said Mikey.

"Why not?" said Norm.

"Thought you'd be grounded."

"Why would I be grounded?" said Norm, even though he knew exactly what Mikey was getting at.

"The tea set?" said Mikey.

"Oh, right!" said Norm. "You mean the tea set that *you* smashed?"

"Technically, yeah," said Mikey.

"What do you mean, *technically*?"

"Well, you know..."

"Don't tell me *you* think it was my fault too, Mikey?"

"No, but..."

"You were the one riding the bike! You smashed it, not me!"

"Smashed what?" said Mikey's dad, emerging from the house, dressed for a run. "Hi, Norman, by the way."

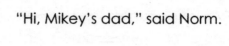

"Hi, Mikey's dad," said Norm.

"How are things?"

"Oh, you know..." said Norm.

"Yeah," said Mikey's dad, nodding sympathetically.

Norm waited for Mikey's dad to carry on, but he never did. Mikey's dad wasn't really one for carrying on. He was laidback. He was cool. He was funny. In other words, thought Norm, the complete opposite of his *own* dad.

"So, Mikey?" said Mikey's dad eventually.

"What, Dad?" said Mikey.

"What did you smash?"

Norm and Mikey exchanged glances.

"My mum's tea set," said Norm.

"Oh, for goodness sake, Mikey!" said Mikey's dad.

"Actually it used to be my grandma's," said Norm.

"Aw, you're joking!" said Mikey's dad.

"I wish!" said Norm.

"Your mum must be devastated, Norman."

"Actually she didn't want to talk about it."

"Hmm. Probably too upset."

"Dunno, maybe," said Norm wishing that Mikey's dad would hurry up and go for his flipping run. The sooner he did, the sooner he and Mikey could get off on their bikes. And by the looks of things it was about to rain.

"What about your grandpa?" said Mikey's dad. "Have you told him yet?"

"Yeah," said Norm.

"And...?"

"He wasn't bothered," said Norm.

"Maybe not on the outside," said Mikey's dad. "But he'll be hurting on the inside."

"No really, he's not bothered," said Norm. "He said it was just stuff and that he doesn't need any more stuff cos he's nearly dead."

"And this was your fault was it, Mikey?" said Mikey's dad.

"Kind of," said Mikey as the first drops of rain began to fall.

"*Kind* of?" said Mikey's dad.

Mikey sighed. He too was beginning to wish his dad would hurry up and go for his flipping run.

"It was my fault," said Mikey.

"Well, I'm really sorry, Norman," said Mikey's dad.

"Honestly, it's fine," said Norm, as the rain began to fall harder and harder.

"No, it's not, it's not fine at all," said Mikey's dad, finally setting off. "I'll talk to you about this later, Mikey!"

By the time Mikey's dad had reached the end of the drive, the rain was bouncing off the pavement. Norm and Mikey looked at each other, both thinking exactly the same thing, both wishing that the other would hurry up and suggest it.

"Computer?" said Mikey at last.

"Oh, come on, Mikey! It's just a drop of rain!" said Norm.

"You call *this* a drop of rain?" said Mikey looking up at the sky.

But there was no reply. Norm had already leaned his bike against the wall and was halfway to the front door.

CHAPTER 14

"There you go boys," said Mikey's
mum, plonking down two huge
mugs of hot chocolate next to
the computer. "Just the way
you like it, Norman. Squirty
cream and a flake on top!"

"Thanks, Mikey's mum," said
Norm.

"Yeah, thanks, Mum, that's magic,"
said Mikey.

"Your dad needs his head examining going out
in this, if you ask me," said Mikey's mum, looking
out the window, where it was still chucking it down
with rain. "Or even if you don't ask me."

Mikey and his mum laughed. Norm would've joined in too if he hadn't just taken his first mouthful of hot chocolate. For one delicious moment Norm thought he'd died and gone to heaven.

"Is that OK, Norman?" said Mikey's mum.

"No, it's not OK," said Norm.

Mikey's mum looked at Norm.

"It's *amazing!*" said Norm, grinning from ear to ear.

Mikey's mum smiled. "What are you boys looking at anyway? Nothing inappropriate I hope!"

"Course not, Mum," said Mikey.

"That's good," laughed Mikey's mum.

Nothing ever seemed to bother Mikey's mum, thought Norm. She was always so nice and understanding. Plus she made the most phenomenal hot chocolate. Norm took another sip of hot chocolate and for a few seconds all was well with the world.

"Penny for your thoughts, Norman," said Mikey's mum.

"Sorry, what?" said Norm.

"You seem a bit distracted."

Norm couldn't very well say what was *really* on his mind. That he wished *his* mum was more like Mikey's.

"How's your mum by the way?"

"Compared to you, you mean?" said Norm without thinking.

"Pardon?" said Mikey's mum.

"Er, I mean she's fine, thanks," said Norm.

"And your dad?"

Again, what was Norm supposed to say? That his dad seemed more concerned with a dog doing a dump in the house than the fact that at this rate they might not *have* a house for that much longer?

"He's all right, I s'pose," said Norm.

"Say hello to them for me, won't you?"

"Yeah, course," said Norm, secretly hoping that he wouldn't have an opportunity to actually do that for a good while. Secretly wishing that he could swap parents, like on some kind of reality TV show. Not permanently. Maybe just for a couple of weeks or so. Just to give him a taste of what it would be like to be part of a *normal* family.

"Well, I'd better leave you boys to it, then," said Mikey's mum, heading for the door. "Is there anything else you want?"

"How long have you got?" blurted Norm.

"Sorry, Norman?"

"Er, I said how long have we got, Mikey's mum?" said Norm. "On the computer I mean?"

"As long as you want, Norman!" laughed Mikey's mum. "Mi casa, su casa!"

"Pardon?" said Norm.

"It's Spanish," said Mikey's mum disappearing out of the door. "It means 'my house is your house'!"

"If only," muttered Norm under his breath.

Mikey looked at Norm. "I know what you're thinking, Norm."

"I doubt it," said Norm.

"They're not perfect."

Norm pulled a face. "Who aren't?"

"My parents," said Mikey. "I know you think they're really great and that we never argue and stuff. But we do!"

"I don't know what you're talking about, Mikey."

But of course, Norm knew *exactly* what Mikey was talking about. He just didn't want Mikey to *know* that he knew what he was talking about. Besides, it was pretty hard to believe that Mikey and his parents ever argued. They were obviously loaded. What could they possibly have to argue about?

Mikey looked at Norm.

"What?" said Norm, irritably.

"Nothing," said Mikey. "YouTube?"

"Whatever," said Norm.

"Bike wipe outs?" said Mikey, tapping away at the keyboard without bothering to wait for an answer.

"Don't mind," said Norm.

Within seconds, Norm and Mikey were watching a clip of a guy jumping off a flight of concrete steps on his bike. It wasn't the jumping off bit that proved to be the problem. It was the landing bit that proved to be the problem. Bike and guy promptly parted company – bike going one way and guy the other.

"Ooooooh!" winced Mikey. "That's gotta hurt!"

"Served him right," muttered Norm.

"What?" said Mikey.

"Served him right."

"Why?" said Mikey.

"Just did," said Norm. "Budge over. I'm gonna leave a comment."

Mikey budged over and watched as Norm typed.

"  ?" said Mikey.

"Yeah?" said Norm.

"Laugh out loud?"

"Yeah? So?"

"I'd like to see *you* do that, Norm!"

"And I suppose you *could*, could you?" Norm shot back.

They looked at each other for a moment, both knowing that if it came to the crunch, Mikey most likely *could* do it.

"Probably not, no," said Mikey.

Norm clicked on another clip – this time one of a mountain biker failing to negotiate a bend in the track and crashing straight into a tree.

"Ouch!" said Mikey, as Norm immediately began posting another comment.

"Loser?" read Mikey. "What is *wrong* with you today, Norm?"

"Nothing," said Norm, already downloading another clip.

"Do you want to talk about it?" said Mikey.

"Talk about it?" laughed Norm. "What am I? A girl or something?"

"I just thought..." Mikey suddenly stopped mid-sentence, his eyes fixed on the screen.

"What is it?" said Norm.

"Play that one again," said Mikey.

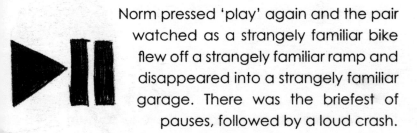 Norm pressed 'play' again and the pair watched as a strangely familiar bike flew off a strangely familiar ramp and disappeared into a strangely familiar garage. There was the briefest of pauses, followed by a loud crash.

"Oops," muttered a strangely familiar voice.

"Ow," groaned another strangely familiar voice from within the strangely familiar garage.

"Aaaaaaaand cut!" said a third voice.

Norm stared at the screen in a state of shock. Who the heck did the girl next door think she was, filming him and Mikey and then posting it on YouTube?

"Well?" said Mikey.

"Well, what?" said Norm.

"Gonna leave a comment?" said Mikey.

Leave a comment? thought Norm. Oh, he was going to leave a comment all right! He was going to leave a comment so cutting and witheringly witty the flipping girl next door wouldn't know what had flipping well hit her!

"Whoa!" said Mikey.

"What?" said Norm, trying to think of something suitably cutting and witheringly witty.

"It's had over a thousand hits already!"

"What has?" said Mikey's dad, appearing in the doorway, looking like a drowned rat.

"Nothing, Dad," said Mikey.

"Hi Mikey's dad," said Norm.

"Hi Norman, I was hoping you'd still be here."

"Were you?" said Norm.

"Yeah," said Mikey's dad. "I've got something for you."

"Really?" said Norm. "What's that?"

"A hundred pounds," said Mikey's dad, holding out a wad of folded-up banknotes.

Norm opened his mouth to say something but nothing came out. A hundred quid? A hundred flipping quid? Just think what he could do with that!

"Norman?" said Mikey's dad. "Are you OK?"

But Norm had temporarily lost the power of speech.

"I know your mum will never actually be able to *replace* it," said Mikey's dad.

"Sorry?" said Norm, suddenly rediscovering the power of speech. "Replace what?"

"The tea set," said Mikey's dad. "You didn't think I was just giving you a hundred pounds did you, Norman?"

"What?" said Norm. "No, course I didn't! I was just thinking how amazingly generous of you that is, Mikey's dad."

Mikey sniggered. He knew that Norm hadn't so much got hold of the wrong *end* of the stick, as missed the stick altogether.

"I don't know what *you're* laughing at Mikey," said Mikey's dad. "That's your pocket money for the next twenty weeks that is!"

 " said Mikey.

"You heard," said Mikey's dad.

It was Norm's turn to snigger.

CHAPTER 15

Norm didn't *deliberately* not give his mum the money for the tea set, it just kind of happened. Or rather, it just kind of *didn't* happen. Norm *meant* to give it to her, but by the time he'd got back from Mikey's it was time for dinner and then it was time for the usual argument about not doing the washing up, followed by the usual argument about always leaving his homework till Sunday night. Before he knew it, Norm was on the computer, drooling over new bikes.

It wasn't as if Norm hadn't got a good bike already. He had a perfectly good bike – apart from slightly scratched front forks, that was. But that didn't stop Norm fantasising about buying the bike of his dreams in the unlikely event that he could ever afford to. Which was precisely what he was doing when Brian suddenly appeared behind him.

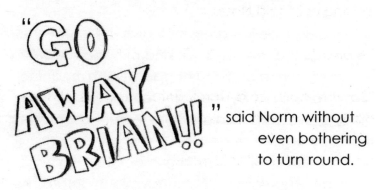 " said Norm without even bothering to turn round.

"How did you know I was here?" said Brian.

"Smelt you," said Norm.

"Ha ha," said Brian.

It wasn't strictly true of course. Norm hadn't smelt Brian, he'd actually heard him when he stepped on the creaky floorboard.

"Are you still there?" said Norm, knowing full well that Brian hadn't budged a millimetre.

"What's that you're looking at?" said Brian, peering over Norm's shoulder.

"Aardvarks.com! What does it *look* like I'm flipping looking at?" said Norm.

"A bike."

"So why ask?" said Norm, irritation levels already dangerously high.

"Dunno. Just did," said Brian.

Norm sighed with exasperation. "Brian?"

"Go away."

"Whoa!" said Brian. "That is seriously expensive!"

Norm sighed again.

"Brian?"

"Yeah?"

"Which part of 'go away' do you not understand?"

"Oh, I forgot to tell you," said Brian, still showing no signs of budging. "I've got a message from Mum."

Norm clicked on 'Parts and Accessories'. If he couldn't afford a whole new bike, the next best thing was to pimp up his current bike. Not that he could afford to do that either. But there was no harm in looking.

"And?" said Norm.

"And what?" said Brian.

"What's the flipping message?" yelled Norm.

"No need to shout," said Brian.

Norm took a deep breath and clicked on a picture of some front forks.

"What's the message from Mum please, Brian?"

"She said to get off the computer and do your homework."

"In a minute," said Norm, as a slightly bigger picture of the forks popped up along with some blurb to read.

"What's that?" said Brian.

"Front forks," said Norm through firmly gritted teeth.

"But you've got some already."

"I *need* some new ones," hissed Norm menacingly.

"Why?"

"Because I just do!" screamed Norm. "Now clear off!"

But even as he said it, Norm knew that he was wasting his breath. His brothers were like midges. Swatting them away made no difference whatsoever. They just kept coming back. If Norm *really* wanted some peace and quiet, then he was going to have to try some new tactics.

"I saw that dog by the way."

"Simon Cowell?" said Brian, brightening immediately. "Where?"

"By the side of the road," said Norm.

Brian's face dropped.

"What do you mean, 'by the side of the road'?"

Norm paused. It was payback time. He was determined to enjoy this.

"Got hit by a car."

"What?" shrieked Brian, his eyes welling up with tears.

"I'm kidding," said Norm.

"What do you mean?" said Brian.

Norm paused again.

"He didn't get hit by a car."

Brian sighed an enormous sigh of relief.

"It was a lorry," said Norm.

"What?" shrieked Brian.

"I'm kidding," said Norm.

Brian waited, his face frozen somewhere between hope and hysteria.

"It was a bus," said Norm, grinning.

That did the trick. Brian ran out of the room screaming, finally leaving Norm alone. Norm knew he'd get into trouble, but he didn't care. It would be worth it for a few minutes' peace.

The front forks, as Norm discovered, were on special offer – reduced from £120 to £60. Norm did a quick mental calculation. Including the £10 that Grandpa had given him yesterday, he now had the grand total of – well, £10. That still didn't stop Norm clicking 'Add to basket' and looking at other stuff he could buy if he ever had the money. He found the whole process of creating his dream bike somehow liberating and comforting. It enabled Norm to forget about all the things he was only too happy to forget about.

$$£120 \\ -£60 \over £60$$ $- 10 =$

For a little while anyway.

"What's all this about Simon Cowell getting run over?" said Norm's mum from the doorway.

"It was a joke, Mum!"

"A joke?"

"He was annoying me!"

"Who? Simon Cowell?"

"No. Brian."

"So you deliberately upset him?"

"Yeah?" shrugged Norm. "What's wrong with that?"

Norm's mum looked at Norm.

"What, Mum? It was funny!"

"You call pretending a dog's been run over by a bus, *funny*?"

Norm smiled as he remembered the look of horror on Brian's face. His only regret was not taking a picture and using it as a screensaver.

"Anyway your dad and I have decided to get one."

Norm was confused.

"What? A bus?"

"No," said Norm's mum. "A dog."

"What?"

"For your brothers."

Norm had heard the expression 'having the wind taken out of your sails', but he'd never really understood what it meant. Until now.

"We've been talking it over," continued Norm's mum. "We think they've found the whole moving thing a bit difficult to deal with. We think a dog might help take their minds off it."

"But..."

"I know," said Norm's mum. "I can't say I'm crazy about the idea myself. I dread to think of the mess! But well – as long as Brian and Dave are happy, that's all that matters I suppose."

Never mind having the wind taken out of his sails, Norm felt like he'd just struck an iceberg and was about to sink.

"But..."

"But *what* Norm?" said Norm's mum.

There were so *many* buts, Norm didn't know where to start. Luckily he didn't have to, because at that moment there was a beep from the computer.

Someone was trying to contact him on msn. Norm opened up the message. It was from Mikey.

Dad says have you given your mum the money yet?

X reply

read Norm's mum.
"What money's that then, Norman?"

Norm was still so gobsmacked that he forgot to be miffed with his mum for reading the message over his shoulder.

"Oh yeah, sorry. Forgot, Mum. For the tea set."

"Really?" said Norm's mum. "That's very sweet of Mikey's dad, but he shouldn't have."

Actually he *should* have, thought Norm, his mind immediately whirring into overdrive. So his stupid little brothers had found moving house *difficult* had they? Well boo flipping hoo! What about Norm? How did his parents think *he* flipping well felt? What

158

flipping planet were they *from* exactly?

"How much?" said Norm's mum.

Norm knew that if he was going to do it then he just had to do it. He couldn't afford to think about it or hesitate. It was now or never.

"How much, love?" repeated Norm's mum.

How much more would he need for the forks? thought Norm.

"Fifty pounds please, Mum," said Norm.

Norm's mum pulled a face. "What do you mean, *please*?"

"Er, nothing," said Norm quickly, desperately hoping his mum couldn't hear his heart pounding like a drum against his chest.

CHAPTER 16

Norm took ages to get to sleep that night. Not because he was kept awake by his dad's snoring. Not because he'd almost peed in a wardrobe – or any other item of furniture for that matter. Norm took ages to get to sleep that night because he was just too excited. He could still hardly believe what he'd done. His mind was buzzing like a hyperactive bluebottle. Sleep was way down Norm's list of stuff to do.

Norm knew deep down that what he'd done was wrong. But *so* deep down it didn't really matter. Norm had felt so incensed and hard done by at the time that he genuinely believed fifty pounds was the very *least* he deserved. Frankly, thought Norm, his mum was lucky to be getting *that* much. And besides, it was never his intention to simply take the money and forget all about it. He liked to think of it more as a loan. Norm fully intended to pay it back sooner or later. Preferably later.

Norm's mind was still buzzing when he came down for breakfast the next morning.

"Hey, guess what, Norman?" blurted Brian, spraying a mouthful of own-brand coco pops all over the table.

"You're getting a dog," said Norm.

"How did you know?" said Dave.

"Mum told me," said Norm. "Didn't you, Mum?"

Norm's mum smiled and nodded.

"What do you think, Norman?" said Norm's dad.

"What do I think, Dad?" said Norm. "I think it's a great idea!"

"Really?" said Norm's dad, slightly surprised.

"Absolutely! Like Mum said – as long as Brian and Dave are happy that's all that matters!"

Norm's mum and dad exchanged a quick glance.

"Well I must say, Norman, that's a very mature attitude," said Norm's dad.

"Well, I *am* nearly thirteen, Dad!" laughed Norm.

"We're going to call it Jesus if it's a boy," said Dave.

"Or maybe Simon Cowell," said Brian. "We've not decided yet."

"Cool," said Norm.

"My word," said Norm's mum. "*Someone's* got out of bed the right side this morning."

"What do you mean, Mum?" said Norm.

"Well it's just that you didn't seem very keen on the idea last night, love."

"That was before..." began Norm.

"Before what?" said Norm's mum.

Norm hesitated. What should he say? Certainly not the truth.

"Er, before I realised that it's actually a really good idea, Mum!"

Norm's mum smiled. "I'm glad you think so, love."

Brian and Dave, meanwhile, finished their breakfast and disappeared upstairs, jabbering excitedly to each other.

"I know about the money by the way, Norman," said Norm's dad.

"What, Dad?" said Norm, visions of brand new front forks already beginning to evaporate. Was it really that obvious that he was up to something?

"I said I know about the money," repeated Norm's dad.

"What money, Dad?" said Norm as casually as possible.

"The money for the tea set?" said Norm's dad. "The fifty pounds that Mikey's dad gave you?"

"Oh, *that* money!" said Norm.

Norm's dad looked puzzled. "Yeah, of course. Why?"

"Er, nothing, Dad," said Norm quickly. "It's just a bit early that's all! I'm still half asleep!"

Norm yawned theatrically and began tucking into his cereal. Had he got away with it? he wondered.

"We can't accept it, Norman," said Norm's dad.

"What do you mean, Dad?" said Norm, almost choking on a mouthful of own-brand cornflakes.

"We're not *that* hard up," said Norm's dad. "We don't need charity!"

"I don't think Mikey's dad meant it like that, Alan," said Norm's mum.

"How do *you* know what he meant it like?" snapped Norm's dad. "Were you there?"

"No," said Norm's mum quietly.

"Well then," said Norm's dad.

Norm looked at his mum. She looked like she was about to cry.

"I was there, Dad," said Norm.

"What?" said Norm's dad irritably.

"I was there," repeated Norm. "I just think Mikey's dad felt bad about the tea set, that's all. I don't think he was feeling sorry for us or anything."

Norm's mum looked at Norm and tried to smile gratefully.

"How would he even *know* that things were – you know…"

"Tricky?" prompted Norm's mum.

"Yeah," said Norm. "How would he know that?"

166

"I don't care," said Norm's dad. "We still can't take it. You're going to have to give it back, Norman."

"It was very kind of him though, love," said Norm's mum.

But Norm's mum might as well have been talking Swedish. Norm wasn't listening anymore. His mind was whirring into overdrive again. What if he *didn't* give the money back to Mikey's dad? All of a sudden Norm wouldn't just have *fifty* pounds – he'd have a *hundred*! Plus the ten pounds from Grandpa! Norm would be rich beyond his wildest dreams!

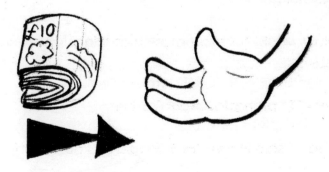

"What are you thinking, love?" said Norm's mum.

"Sorry, Mum, what?" said Norm, suddenly snapping out of it.

"What are you thinking?"

"Oh, just – you know, that you're right, Mum," said Norm. "It *was* very kind of Mikey's dad to give me the money. I mean, give *you* the money. For the tea set. Not for anything else. Obviously."

"Here," said Norm's dad, holding out the same wad of folded-up banknotes that Norm had given his mum the night before.

Norm stared at the money, thinking of all the stuff he'd be able to buy for his bike now.

"Well, go on then," said Norm's dad. "Take it."

With pleasure, thought Norm, taking the money and pocketing it. With absolute pleasure.

CHAPTER 17

Norm found it hard to concentrate at school that day. Or rather, Norm found it even harder than *usual* to concentrate at school that day. It never took much to derail Norm's train of thought, but that particular morning he found it virtually impossible to stay on track. It was hardly surprising. Norm's mind was still buzzing so much he half expected someone to ask him to keep the noise down.

Norm could still hardly believe what he'd done. But there was no going back now. He'd decided. He was borrowing the money. The whole hundred pounds. And even if there was a way of going back, Norm figured he'd probably get into trouble now anyway, so he might as well spend it.

The only problem, thought Norm
– gazing out the window at a
plane leaving a vapour trail
across the sky, like freshly
squeezed toothpaste –
was *how* to spend the
money? How was
he actually
going to buy
the stuff
to pimp
his bike up
with *without*
his parents finding
out? OK, so as problems
went it was a relatively *nice* problem. It wasn't like
he'd just been given forty-eight hours to save the
world, using only string and a yoghurt container or
something. But nevertheless it was still a problem.

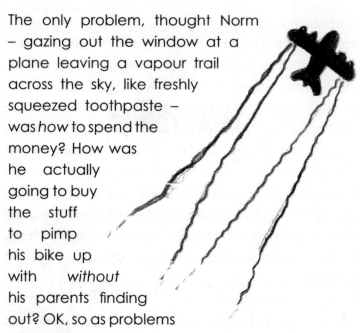

The special offer on the front forks was exclusive
to the website that Norm had found them on. He
was going to have to buy them online. In order to
buy something online you needed a
card. The only kind of card that
Norm had was a library card

and he was pretty sure he wouldn't be able to use that. No, thought Norm, one way or another he was going to have to get his hands on a debit card. His mum obviously had one. How else could she buy all that stuff from the shopping channels? His dad obviously had one too. Whether there was actually any money left in his bank account was another matter entirely. But that didn't matter. Norm would somehow deposit the hundred pounds into the account and hope his parents didn't notice. And *then* hope they didn't notice when a whacking great parcel suddenly turned up a couple of days later!

Come to think of it, thought Norm, that was *another* problem. Where should he get the stuff delivered to if he didn't want his mum and dad to find out? And where was he going to fit it? In fact never mind *where* was he going to fit it – *how* was he going to fit it? He'd need help. He'd need tools. He'd need a flipping miracle at this rate!

The more Norm thought about it, the more he realised there wasn't only *one* problem to overcome, there was a whole *bunch* of problems. And that was *without* thinking about potentially the *biggest* problem of all, lurking round the corner like a bad smell. How the heck was Norm *ever* going to find a hundred pounds to pay Mikey's dad back? There was more chance of Norm getting a half-decent school report. And there was no chance of that! Besides this problem, the other problems paled into insignificance. The other problems were merely starters. This was the main course. This was a super-sized problem with a side order of trouble.

"Earth to Norman, come in please, Norman!" said a voice from a galaxy far, far away.

"Sorry? What, Mum?" said Norm, turning round to find Miss Evans, his French teacher, standing next to him. "I mean, Miss."

But it was too late. The damage had been done.

Norm could already feel himself burning up with embarrassment even before the class erupted into gales of laughter. Everyone was staring at him and grinning. Everyone that is, except Mikey.

"All right, you lot!" said Mikey. "It's no big deal! We've all done it!"

"Thank you, Michael," said Miss Evans. "Now carry on with your work everybody. Show's over."

Norm glanced at Mikey and immediately felt a twinge of guilt. Mikey might not have been *quite* so quick to stick up for him if he'd known what he was planning to do with his dad's money. Then again, thought Norm, knowing Mikey, he would have *still* stuck up for him even if he *had* known. Mikey was just *so* nice. There wasn't a bad bone in his body. It was *so* flipping annoying!

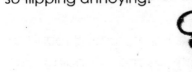

"Norman?"

"Yes, Miss?"

"Is something troubling you?"

"No, Miss."

"Right, well when I said that everybody should carry on with their work, that included you."

"Yes, Miss."

Norm tried to carry on but it wasn't easy, especially as he had no idea what he was actually supposed to be carrying on with. It was French. Norm knew that much. But beyond that it was a bit hazy. He couldn't very well ask now. It was almost the end of the period. He'd have to ask Mikey later. In fact knowing Mikey he'd probably offer to let Norm copy his notes. Good old Mikey. Always there when you needed him.

Thank goodness he'd only moved house and not school as well, thought Norm. At least he and Mikey still saw each other every day. It was the one small crumb of comfort in Norm's otherwise crumb-free world.

Norm glanced at his friend and immediately felt another twinge of guilt. But it soon passed. Before he knew it, Norm was miles away again, riding his newly pimped-up bike to victory in the World Mountain Biking Championships for the seventh year in a row.

CHAPTER 18

"Thanks, Mikey," said Norm.

"What for?" said Mikey.

"Earlier on," said Norm. "I owe you one."

"Do you?" said Mikey, puzzled.

"For sticking up for me?" said Norm.

It was morning break. Norm and Mikey were walking round the playing field eating crisps – vintage farmhouse cheddar and shallots in Mikey's case, supermarket own-brand cheese and onion in Norm's.

"Oh, you mean when you called Miss Evans Mu—"

"Ssshhh! Keep your voice down!" hissed Norm, looking around anxiously. "I don't want the whole flipping school to know!"

Norm needn't have worried. There was no one else within a hundred-metre radius.

"It's no big deal Norm," said Mikey. "We've all done it."

"Yeah, I know," said Norm. "But most people do it when they're like, six or something – not when they're nearly thirteen!"

They looked at each other and grinned.

"Anyway, I still owe you one," said Norm, thinking about the money – which, in a roundabout way, he was actually borrowing from Mikey. "Actually I owe you more than one."

"What are you on about, Norm?"

"The pocket money?" said Norm.

"Oh right, I see," said Mikey. "Don't worry about it. Dad changed his mind after you'd gone.

"What do you mean?"

"He's let me off. I don't have to pay it back any more."

"How come?" said Norm. "It was *your* fault, Mikey!"

"Yeah, I know, but I didn't *mean* to do it," said Mikey. "It was an accident."

A very *fortunate* accident too, thought Norm, if there *was* such a thing as a fortunate accident. Because if Mikey *hadn't* crash landed on the tea set, he wouldn't currently have a hundred and ten pounds burning a hole in his pocket – or stashed under his mattress anyway.

"By the way, have you seen how many hits it's had?" said Mikey.

"How many hits *what's* had?" said Norm.

"The crash," said Mikey.

What with one thing and another, Norm had completely forgotten about the girl next door filming Mikey wiping out and then posting it on YouTube.

"How many?" said Norm.

"Over ten thousand the last time I looked," said Mikey.

"In two days?" said Norm.

"Yeah," said Mikey.

"And how many of those hits are *yours*, Mikey?"

Mikey thought for a moment. "About fifty? But it's still pretty amazing when you think about it, Norm! People from all over the world have seen it! There are loads of comments. There's even one in Japanese!"

"What does it say?" said Norm.

"I've got no idea," said Mikey.

Norm suddenly remembered. He never did leave a comment himself. He was *going* to write something cutting and witheringly witty to make the girl next door pay for it, but then Mikey's dad had walked in and he hadn't given it another thought. Until now...

The idea hit Norm like a bolt from the blue. Never mind leaving a comment. There was another way the girl next door could pay for it. *Literally* pay for it! Norm could give the money to *her* – and *she* could buy the stuff for his bike! It was genius! What could possibly go wrong?

"Oi! Norman!" shouted a voice.

Norm and Mikey turned round to see some kids from the year above walking towards them.

"What do you call your mum then?" said one of them. "Miss?"

The kids all burst out laughing. So much for not wanting the whole school to know. It looked like the whole school knew already.

CHAPTER 19

Norm was straight out on the drive as soon as he got back from school that day. In fact for the next few days Norm spent every spare moment he had out on the drive either riding his bike, cleaning his bike, or fiddling about with it for no reason whatsoever. He only went in the house to eat, sleep, or go to the toilet and frankly if Norm could have done that on the drive he probably would have done. He was a man with a mission. He was desperate to see the girl next door again.

It wasn't until the following Saturday that his patience was finally rewarded.

All right, **NORMAN?**

said a voice from the other side of the fence.

Norm tried to act cool and as if he hadn't been waiting almost a week for this moment to arrive. He also tried not to be *too* irritated by the way the girl next door deliberately overemphasised his name, like it was the funniest thing she'd ever heard. Now that the moment *had* finally arrived, Norm couldn't afford to blow it.

"All right?"

Norm was practising balancing on his bike without actually going anywhere. It was a skill known as a track stand. His current record stood at nine seconds.

"What's the point of that?" said the girl next door.

What's the *point*? thought Norm, wobbling and putting his foot down. There were so many things he wanted to say, but couldn't, no matter how tempting it was. He absolutely had to remain calm if he wanted his plan to work.

"Just practising," said Norm.

The girl laughed.

"What's so funny?" said Norm.

"Nothing," said the girl. "I was just thinking, that's all."

"What?" said Norm.

"You don't *look* like a Norman."

Norm took a deep breath. What exactly was someone called Norman supposed to look like? he wondered.

"Don't I? Sorry."

"It's OK!" said the girl. "You don't have to apologise!"

You're flipping right I don't, thought Norm.

"So what's *your* name?" he said as pleasantly as possible under the circumstances.

"Chelsea," said the girl. "And don't even *think* about it!"

"Don't even think about what?" said Norm.

"Making any jokes."

"I wasn't going to."

"Good, because I've heard them all. And before you ask – no, I *don't* support them!"

"Who?"

The girl pulled a face.

"What are you? Stupid or something?"

Norm's patience was like an elastic band being stretched to breaking point. Any second now it was going to snap.

"My dad does though."

"Your dad does what?" said Norm.

"Supports Chelsea."

"Oh right, I see."

"Could've been worse, I suppose."

"What do you mean?" said Norm.

"He could've supported Arsenal."

Norm couldn't help smiling. For someone so annoying, Chelsea was actually quite funny.

"I don't even *like* football," said Chelsea.

"Me neither," said Norm.

"That's *one* thing we have in common then."

Yeah, probably the *only* thing as well, thought Norm.

"Haven't seen you around much," he said.

"You been looking then?" grinned Chelsea.

"No!" said Norm a bit too quickly.

"I'm only here at weekends," explained Chelsea. "It's my dad's house."

"Right," said Norm.

"I live with my mum the rest of the time."

This was all very fascinating, thought Norm, but when would he get the chance to change the subject?

"Where's your mate by the way?" said Chelsea.

"You mean Mikey?"

"Yeah. Quite a star! Fifty thousand hits and rising!"

This was it, thought Norm. The opportunity he'd been waiting for!

"Actually I've been meaning to talk to you about that," said Norm.

"Oh yeah?" said Chelsea.

"Yeah," said Norm.

Norm hesitated.

"I'm on the edge of my seat," said Chelsea.

Norm had thought about virtually nothing else for the past few days. Time and time again he'd gone over what he was going to say in his head. But now he was going to have to say it out loud. All of a sudden Norm wasn't so sure it was such a good idea. Chelsea was annoying and funny. But was she gullible too?

"The thing is..." began Norm.

"What?" grinned Chelsea. "What's the thing, *Norman*?"

"It's illegal."

"What is?"

"To film someone and then post it on YouTube – without their permission."

Norm hadn't got a clue whether what he'd just said was true or not. He'd made it up. It *sounded* like it could be true though. The question was – would Chelsea fall for it?

"Yeah, right," said Chelsea.

"I'm serious!" said Norm. "It's a security thing!"

"You're having a laugh!" said Chelsea.

"I'm not," said Norm. "People in Japan have seen inside our garage!"

"What, and you think they're going to come all this way and nick some paint do you?"

"They might," said Norm.

"So what are you gonna do about it?" said Chelsea.

"Actually there's something *you* can do for *me*," said Norm.

"Oh yeah?" said Chelsea. "And what's that then?"

Norm looked around to make sure they were still alone. His dad and brothers were out and his mum was no doubt glued to the TV, buying an electric banana straightener or something equally useless.

"Buy some stuff for me. Online."

"What?" said Chelsea.

"Get me some stuff to pimp my bike up with."

"Why can't *you* do it?" said Chelsea.

"Long story," said Norm.

"I've got all day," said Chelsea.

"Will you do it, or won't you?" said Norm, looking around again and getting slightly agitated.

"All right, all right! Calm down, *Norman*!"

Chelsea appeared to mull things over for a few moments.

"I presume you've got the money?"

"Yeah, course I have," said Norm.

"Cash?"

"Cash."

"All I have to do is order it?"

"Simple," said Norm.

"Hmmm."

Why couldn't she hurry up and give him a flipping answer? thought Norm. Unless she was doing it on purpose to keep him in suspense? If she was, it was flipping well working! Norm felt like he was on *The X Factor*, waiting to see if he was about to get booted off or not. All that was missing was the dramatic music.

"What's in it for me?" said Chelsea.

"What do you mean?" said Norm.

"I mean, what's it worth?" said Chelsea. "Apart from you not reporting me to the YouTube police or whatever?"

Norm was flabbergasted. He'd thought that he was the one in control. He'd thought that he was the one calling all the shots. But it seemed he was wrong.

"Er…" said Norm.

"Look, I'll do it, no problem," said Chelsea. "It'll be a laugh. I'll use my mum's card. She'll never even notice. But it'll cost you."

"But…" said Norm.

"I'm not doing it for nothing!" said Chelsea. "What do you take me for?"

Norm decided that it was probably best he didn't say what he took Chelsea for at that moment. At least it looked like she believed the YouTube thing.

"I'll give you five pounds," said Norm.

"Ten," shot back Chelsea.

"What?" said Norm.

"You heard," said Chelsea. "Deal or no deal?"

Norm sighed. If that was the price he was going to have to pay then what the heck? It still left him a hundred pounds to pimp his bike up with. It was better than nothing. *Much* better than nothing!

"Deal or no deal, *Norman*?" said Chelsea.

"Deal," said Norm.

"Do you want to phone a friend?" said Chelsea.

"I said deal, didn't I?" said Norm.

"Excellent!" said Chelsea. "Chelsea one – *Norman* nil!"

"Very funny," said Norm.

"First sign of madness, that," said a voice from the bottom of the drive.

"Oh hi, Grandpa," said Norm swivelling round. "What is?"

"Talking to yourself," said Grandpa.

"I wasn't," said Norm.

"Really?" said Grandpa. "It looked like you were."

"No, honestly I was talking to..."

Norm turned round again, but Chelsea had vanished.

"Oh," said Norm.

"What?" said Grandpa.

"She's gone."

"*She?*" said Grandpa mischievously, his eyes crinkling ever so slightly in the corners. "You got a girlfriend, Norman?"

"No!" said Norm. "Course I haven't!"

Norm could feel himself beginning to blush. He needed to change the subject and he needed to change it fast. "So what brings you here, Grandpa?"

"Just passing by," said Grandpa. "On my way to the allotments."

Norm thought for a moment.

"The allotments!" he said, the seeds of another idea starting to sprout.

But this time Norm really was talking to himself. Grandpa was already halfway down the street.

"Wait for me, Grandpa!" shouted Norm, pedalling down the drive as fast as he could.

CHAPTER 20

It might have been embarrassing at the time, but Grandpa turning up when he did proved to be a real stroke of luck. Not only had Norm figured out *how* to buy the stuff for his bike, it now looked like he'd figured out *where* he could fit it! The shed on Grandpa's allotment! It was perfect! Why on earth hadn't he thought of that before?

Each allotment had its own shed. Some were painted bright colours. Some had verandas. One or two even had satellite dishes. Grandpa's shed though just looked like any old common or garden shed. From the outside anyway.

On the inside it was a different matter altogether. Grandpa's house was even smaller than Norm's, so his shed wasn't just somewhere to store stuff for his allotment in, it was a workshop – somewhere Grandpa came to make things, fix things, or generally potter about. There was a workbench with a vice. There were tools of every description hanging on the walls – each in its own place and arranged according to size. It was all very organised and tidy.

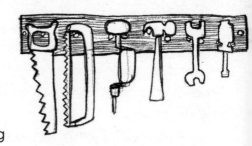

"What's her name then?" said Grandpa, emerging from the shed, weighed down by a huge bag of fertiliser.

"Who?" said Norm, watching him.

"Your girlfriend," said Grandpa, plonking the bag down on the ground and slitting it open with a knife.

198

"I've told you, Grandpa! I haven't got a girlfriend!" said Norm.

"If you say so," said Grandpa.

"I do say so!" said Norm.

"There's nothing wrong with having a girlfriend you know, Norman."

"I know."

"So what's her name – this friend who just happens to be a girl?"

"She's not even a friend!" said Norm. "And her name's Chelsea."

"Chelsea, eh?" said Grandpa. "In a league of her own is she?"

"Shut up, Grandpa!" said Norm.

"I beg your pardon?" said Grandpa.

"I meant shut up, *please*, Grandpa," said Norm.

"That's better," said Grandpa.

"Sorry, Grandpa," said Norm.

"That's OK," said Grandpa. "You've got raging hormones. I understand."

"Grandpa, I have *not* got raging hormones!"

"Maybe not at the moment you haven't," said Grandpa. "But you soon will have. I was your age once. I had raging hormones."

This was way too much information as far as Norm was concerned, but to his enormous relief, Grandpa dropped the subject.

"Make yourself useful and fetch me my radio from the shed."

"'Kay," said Norm.

It was very gloomy inside the shed.
Norm could hardly see a thing.
But then, as if by magic, a single
shaft of sunlight suddenly
pierced the gloom, picking
out Grandpa's radio on the
workbench, like a spotlight
picking out an actor on a
stage.

Norm knew he had to take this opportunity to ask
Grandpa about using the shed. Come to think of
it he'd need to see Chelsea again soon, to tell her
which website to get the forks and the other stuff
from.

"Today sometime!" called Grandpa.

Norm grabbed the radio and headed back
outside.

"Grandpa?"

"What?"

"Can I use your shed?"

Grandpa pulled a face.

"No, you can't! Go on the compost heap like everybody else!"

"I meant – can I use your shed to pimp my bike up?"

"To *what*?" said Grandpa.

"Pimp my bike up," said Norm. "You know – fit new bits to it? And can you help me do it?"

Norm paused.

"Without my mum and dad finding out?"

"Why not?" said Grandpa.

"Aw, that's brilliant!" said Norm. "Thanks, Grandpa!"

"I meant – *why* don't you want your mum and dad to find out?" said Grandpa.

"Oh, I see." Norm sighed.

"Well?" said Grandpa.

"How long have you got?"
said Norm.

Grandpa looked at his watch.
"Five minutes."

"Why?" said Norm. "What's happening
in five minutes?"

"The two thirty at Newmarket," said Grandpa.

This meant absolutely nothing to Norm.

"I've had a little flutter."

"A little what?" said Norm.

"A bet," said Grandpa. "On the two thirty at
Newmarket."

Norm looked puzzled.

"It's a horse race!" said Grandpa. "Don't they teach you *anything* at school these days?"

"So why do you need the radio?" said Norm.

"To listen to the afternoon play," said Grandpa, beginning to get exasperated.

"What?" said Norm.

"To see if I win!" said Grandpa, looking at his watch again. "Four and a half minutes. You'd better get on with it."

Norm took a deep breath and got on with it.

"Mikey's dad gave me a hundred pounds cos Mikey smashed the tea set."

"Did he now?" said Grandpa. "That was very generous of him."

"Yeah, it was," said Norm.

"And...?" said Grandpa.

"I was *supposed* to give it to give to my mum."

"But...?" said Grandpa.

"I didn't."

"I see," said Grandpa.

"I was going to," said Norm.

"But...?" said Grandpa.

Norm hesitated. "I decided to...borrow it instead."

"Hmmm, borrow it, eh? And why was that then, Norman?"

Norm could feel something bubbling and brewing up inside. He couldn't hold it in a second longer and before he knew it, it all came gushing out like verbal diarrhoea.

"Because we've had to move to a stupid little house! Because I'm always getting blamed for stuff my stupid little brothers have done! Because *they're* getting a flipping dog and I'm getting nothing! Because no one seems to care whether *I'm* upset or not! Because we're having to eat super-flipping-market own-brand flipping coco pops! Because Dad's been..."

Norm suddenly remembered he wasn't supposed to tell anyone.

"Your dad's been *what*?" said Grandpa.

What the heck? thought Norm. It wasn't as if Grandpa's opinion of his dad could get much lower.

"Made redundant."

"I see," said Grandpa, beginning to rake fertiliser into the soil.

What was Grandpa thinking? wondered Norm. It was hard to tell.

"I've not *stolen* the money Grandpa! I'm going to pay it back!"

"So you're angry with your dad then."

"What?" said Norm.

"You think this is all your dad's fault?"

"Er, well, yeah, basically," said Norm.

"And that everything's unfair?"

"Yeah," said Norm.

"And that no one understands you?"

"Yeah," said Norm.

"And that the whole world's against you?"

This was starting to get freaky, thought Norm. Was Grandpa psychic or something?

"How do you know all this stuff, Grandpa?"

Grandpa looked at Norm. "Like I said, Norman – I was your age once."

Grandpa looked at his watch. "Don't be too hard on your dad."

Norm was confused. "But I thought you didn't *like* my dad, Grandpa."

"I don't," said Grandpa. "But there are two sides to every story."

"I don't understand," said Norm.

"It's not always a question of one person being right – and the other wrong," said Grandpa. "It's not always that black and white. Sometimes the black and white gets mixed up and makes grey."

Grandpa paused. But Norm didn't want to pause. Norm wanted to fast-forward until the end and

find out what was going to happen.

"Do you understand *now*, Norman?"

Norm didn't really understand but he nodded anyway. "So will you help me then, Grandpa?"

"Course I will," said Grandpa, his eyes crinkling in the corners.

"And you won't say anything to my mum and dad?"

"As long as you pay it back as soon as you can."

Norm's face suddenly broke into a huge grin.

"Don't even *think* about it," said Grandpa.

"About what?" said Norm.

"Hugging me," said Grandpa.

Whoa, thought Norm. Grandpa really *must* be psychic! That's *exactly* what he was going to do!

"Now shut your face and let me listen," said Grandpa, grabbing the radio from Norm and switching it on. But the only sound that came out of it was a low hissing noise.

"Batteries are dead," muttered Grandpa setting off down the path. "Come on, Norman."

Norm picked up his bike and followed. That was another problem crossed off the list then. Everything was falling into place.

CHAPTER 21

"Wait there, Norman," said Grandpa, disappearing through a doorway. "I'll be back in a minute."

"'Kay, Grandpa," said Norm, only too happy to stop and practise his track stands for a while.

Norm didn't think to ask why, at the age of nearly thirteen, he had to wait on the pavement, like a dog outside a butcher's. It never even crossed his mind  that Grandpa might have gone somewhere Norm wasn't actually allowed to be. Then again, Norm hadn't been paying much attention since leaving the allotments. Grandpa could have been abducted by aliens and replaced by a clone and Norm wouldn't have noticed.

Norm's mind was on other things. The puzzle of how to pimp his bike up was gradually being completed, piece by piece like a gigantic jigsaw. Chelsea was going to buy the stuff online for him. It was going to be fitted in Grandpa's shed – and Grandpa was going to help fit it. There was no reason why Norm's mum and dad need ever find out now. And with any luck, they never would.

There was only one piece of the jigsaw left to slot into place before the puzzle was finally finished. What with one thing and another though, Norm

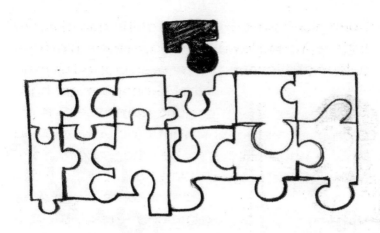

still hadn't thought about how he was ever going to be able to pay Mikey's dad back. But that was just fine by Norm. As long as he didn't actually think about it, it meant that the problem didn't actually exist. Just like if he never thought about brain-sucking zombies from Mars, they didn't exist either. There was one big difference. The problem of how to pay Mikey's dad back was a *real* problem – and a problem that was never going to go away. It was like having a persistent itch in an unmentionable place. Sooner or later, Norm was going to have to scratch it.

"Here you go, Norman," said Grandpa, emerging from the doorway.

Norm wobbled and put his foot down on the ground. His record of a nine-second track stand was safe for now.

"Well, go on then. Take it," said Grandpa, holding out what looked suspiciously like a twenty-pound note.

£20

Norm stared. On closer inspection, it was a twenty-pound note. What was going on? Why was Grandpa offering him money? Had he missed something?

"You can put that towards pumping up your bike or whatever you call it," said Grandpa.

"Pimping up," said Norm.

"That's the one," said Grandpa.

"But..." said Norm.

"I won," said Grandpa.

"Won what?" said Norm.

"The two thirty at Newmarket."

Norm looked confused.

"You don't think I do it for fun do you, Norman?" said Grandpa. "They really *don't* teach you anything at school these days, do they?"

Norm looked up and for the first time, realised where he'd been waiting. "A betting shop?"

"Of course!" said Grandpa. "You didn't think I'd nipped into the library to borrow a book did you?"

That would explain why he'd had to wait outside then, thought Norm. You had to be at least eighteen to go in a betting shop. Norm was nearly thirteen. His face was smoother than a particularly smooth baby's bottom. He could just about pass for fourteen if the lighting was dim and he put on a deep voice. But eighteen? No way, José.

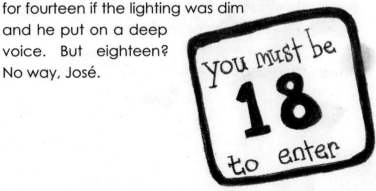

"So you just give them money and if your horse wins you get more money back?"

"Precisely," said Grandpa.

Norm thought for a moment. "How much did you bet, Grandpa?"

"A fiver."

"And you got twenty back?"

"Thirty actually," said Grandpa.

"Whoa!" said Norm. "Thirty pounds just like that?"

"Just like that," said Grandpa. "Pretty good, eh?"

It *was* pretty good, thought Norm. Almost too good to be true, in fact. There *had* to be a catch.

"How do you know which horse is going to win, Grandpa?"

"That's the thing," said Grandpa. "You don't."

Ah, thought Norm. So *that* was the catch.

"You can study the form book and try and work out which one's got the best chance, but at the end of the day you might as well just close your eyes and stick a pin in!"

"Sounds painful," said Norm.

"I mean – stick a pin in the name of a *horse*."

OUCH!!!

"Oh, right," said Norm. "What was the name of *your* horse?"

"Touching Cloth," said Grandpa. "Five to one."

"Five to one?" said Norm. "I thought you said it was the two thirty?"

"Those were the odds," said Grandpa. "Five to one. You bet a pound and you get *five* pounds back if it wins. Plus the original pound."

"Right," said Norm. "So if you bet *five* pounds you get..."

"Twenty-five back," said Grandpa. "Plus the original fiver."

"I see," said Norm.

"But it's a gamble, Norman," said Grandpa. "You win some, you lose some.

But Norm wasn't listening anymore. Not for the first time lately, his mind was whirring into overdrive. Perhaps there *was* a way of paying Mikey's dad back after all. Of course he'd have to ask someone to place the bet *for* him. He couldn't do it himself.

"Talking of winning," said Grandpa, "if you don't take this soon I'm going straight back in there and putting it on another horse. I'm on a roll."

"Thanks very much, Grandpa," said Norm taking the twenty-pound note.

A car horn beeped, but Norm didn't pay any attention. It was only after it beeped three more times that he turned around to see who it was. Without him noticing, Norm's dad had pulled up by the kerb and he didn't look happy.

"What do you think you're doing, Norman?"

"Hi, Grandpa!" yelled Brian from the back of the car.

"Hi, Grandpa!" yelled Dave, sitting next to him.

Grandpa pulled a scary face, but Brian and Dave just laughed.

"I'll see you at home," said Norm's dad, driving off again.

Norm watched the car disappear down the street, his little brothers waving through the back window.

"Course he'll see me at home," said Norm. "Where does he *think* he'll see me?"

"Talking out his backside as usual," said Grandpa.

See you at home

CHAPTER 22

Norm's dad was waiting in the front room when Norm got back. He still didn't look happy.

"Shut the door and sit down, Norman."

Norm shut the door and sat down.

"What were you doing outside the bookies?"

"The what?" said Norm.

"The bookies," said Norm's dad. "The bookmakers."

Norm looked blank.

"The betting shop?"

"Oh, right," said Norm. "Nothing, Dad. I was just waiting for Grandpa, that was all."

"Why?"

"Why was I waiting for Grandpa?" said Norm. "Because he asked me to."

"Why?" said Norm's dad.

"I thought he'd gone to get batteries."

"Batteries?"

"Yeah, for his radio."

"From the bookies?" said Norm's dad.

"I didn't know that's where he'd gone, Dad!"

"How could you not have known where he'd gone?"

"I dunno! I just wasn't concentrating, I suppose."

"You weren't concentrating?" said Norm's dad, increasingly suspicious.

"Well, I mean I was," said Norm. "But on other stuff."

Norm's dad glanced at the door.

"I saw him give you some money, Norman."

Norm hesitated. He had a bad feeling about the way the conversation was headed. One slip now and everything could go seriously pear-shaped.

"Did you?" said Norm.

"How much?" said Norm's dad.

"Twenty pounds."

"Twenty pounds?"

"He won it," said Norm.

"*Grandpa* won it?" said Norm's dad.

Norm nodded.

"*You* didn't?"

"No, Dad."

"You sure?"

"Sure, Dad."

"Promise?"

"Cub's honour, Dad."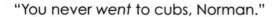

Norm's dad looked at Norm.

"You never *went* to cubs, Norman."

"I did once."

This was true. Norm *had* gone to cubs once, but just the once. Accidentally setting fire to one of the leaders might have had something to do with that. Norm still couldn't see what the all the fuss had been about. They'd put him out hadn't they?

"So you didn't ask Grandpa to bet *for* you then?" said Norm's dad.

"Dad I told you! I never even knew that's where he'd gone!"

"You swear, Norman?"

I will in a flipping minute, thought Norm.

"Because if I ever find out you've..."

Norm's dad stopped mid-sentence like he'd suddenly run out of words.

"What's the matter, Dad?" said Norm.

Norm's dad exhaled slowly and noisily. Whatever the matter was, it was clearly weighing heavily on his mind.

"I wish that I could give you money, Norman."

"I know you do, Dad," said Norm.

Norm's dad suddenly slumped forward and buried his face in his hands.

"Dad?" said Norm. "Are you OK?"

What was going on? wondered Norm. Should he call his mum? Should he call an ambulance? But before he could do either, his dad sat upright again and took a deep breath.

"I didn't resign from my job, Norman."

"I know you didn't," said Norm before he could stop himself.

"What?" said Norm's dad.

"Er, I mean didn't you, Dad?" said Norm, airily.

"I didn't get made redundant either."

Hang on, thought Norm. So if his dad hadn't *resigned* – and he hadn't been made *redundant* – that meant...

"I was fired, Norman," said Norm's dad, saving Norm the bother of having to work it out for himself.

"What?" said Norm.

"I was fired. Sacked. Dismissed. Given the boot."

"But…" said Norm.

"It's a bit like us moving house," said Norm's dad.

"It is?" said Norm, seriously beginning to wonder if his dad was beginning to lose it. Whatever little there was to lose in the first place.

"I didn't leave because I *wanted* to. I left because I *had* to."

"Right," said Norm.

Norm's dad looked relieved. Like whatever had been weighing on his mind had just been lifted.

"There. I've said it."

"Why?" said Norm.

"Because I couldn't keep it bottled up any longer, Norman! I *had* to tell someone! I haven't even told your mum!"

"I meant *why* were you fired, Dad?"

"Oh, I see," said Norm's dad. "Funny you should ask."

"Is it?" said Norm, doubtfully.

"I was caught gambling."

"Gambling?"

Norm was beginning to see why his dad might have been less than thrilled to find him hanging around outside a betting shop.

"Online. Strictly against company rules. They warned me, but I kept on doing it."

Norm's dad glanced at the door again and took another deep breath.

"I lost thousands."

"Of *pounds*?" said Norm in amazement.

"Our entire life savings. Every penny. Gone. Just like that!"

"Whoa!" said Norm.

"I didn't mean to. It just kind of... happened."

Norm didn't understand. How could you not *mean* to gamble away thousands of pounds? Norm hadn't *meant* to nearly pee in his dad's wardrobe. He hadn't *meant* to destroy his mum's tea set. Or at least *Mikey* hadn't meant to. But this was different. This was *way* different!

"So it was an accident?" said Norm.

"Not exactly."

Norm still didn't understand. How could something *not exactly* be an accident? Surely it either was or it wasn't.

"They were talking about getting rid of people."

"They?" said Norm.

"The company," said Norm's dad.

"Right," said Norm.

"I started worrying what would happen if they got rid of *me*. What would I do? How would we manage?"

"You mean..."

"Financially, Norman!"

Norm pulled a face. "Mum's got a job hasn't she?"

"Just as well," said Norm's dad, throwing a meaningful glance in the direction of the TV.

Norm looked. The TV was on mute, but as far as he could tell, a bright orange woman was modelling a ring so huge she could barely lift her arm up. The stone sparkled so brightly under the studio lights, Norm practically had to shield his eyes to prevent being dazzled. Not only that, but the ring was apparently a bargain. If you bought one, you got another one absolutely free.

"Hmmm," said Norm, unsure what else he could say. Apart from hurry up and get to the flipping point!

"So anyway, I was looking at a job website one day – you know, just in case – and this advert popped up."

"Advert?" said Norm.

"For online poker," said Norm's dad. "It said they'd even give you twenty-five pounds to make your first bet!"

"So..." said Norm.

"It seemed silly not to."

"What happened?" said Norm.

"I won," said Norm's dad.

"How much, Dad?"

"Ten pounds."

"And then what?" said Norm.

"I had another bet."

"And you won again?" guessed Norm.

"And again. And again. And again," said Norm's dad. "Before I knew it I'd won five hundred quid!"

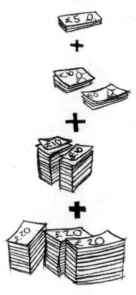

Norm whistled. Five hundred pounds with a few clicks of a mouse? Result!

"I'm not going to lie to you, Norman. It felt fantastic at the time. I thought that if I did end up losing my job I could at least make money by gambling! It was money for nothing!"

Norm could see how his dad might think that. He was thinking pretty much the same thing himself.

"The trouble was..."

Norm couldn't think what the trouble might have been. You bet some money – you won some money. You bet some more money – you won some more money. It seemed like a pretty trouble-free plan to Norm.

"What, Dad?"

"Once I'd started I couldn't stop."

Norm was still struggling to see what the problem was.

"Even when I started to lose," said Norm's dad.

"Lose?"

"Well, of course. You always lose in the end, Norman. You can't keep winning forever! I *thought* I could. I thought I'd got it all under control, but before I knew it, it was the other way round. *It* was controlling *me*. By the time I realised, it was too late."

Norm's dad buried his face in his hands again.

"I've been such an idiot."

Norm couldn't quite decide whether his dad had been an idiot or not. On the one hand he'd blown more money than Norm could possibly imagine. On the other hand he'd genuinely believed that he was doing it for the right reasons. What was that Grandpa had said about there being two sides to every story? About black and white sometimes getting mixed up and making grey?

"I'm not expecting you to understand, Norman."

Norm looked at his dad. "But I think I kind of do, Dad."

"Really?"

"Yeah," said Norm. "But can I ask you something?"

"Go for it."

"Why didn't you tell Mum you'd been fired?"

Norm's dad thought for a moment.

"I guess it was a pride thing."

"A pride thing?"

"I know it sounds crazy," said Norm's dad. "I can't explain."

"Are you *going* to tell her?"

Norm's dad nodded.

"When?" said Norm.

"When the time's right."

Norm wondered whether there was *ever* a right time to tell someone you'd been fired from your job for gambling away your family's savings? It wasn't exactly the sort of thing you could drop into conversation over morning coffee. Probably best to do it by text, decided Norm. Preferably when you were on a different continent.

236

"You won't tell her will you, Norman?"

Norm looked at his dad. Should he? Could he? Would he?

"Please, Norman?"

"What's it worth, Dad?" grinned Norm.

But Norm's dad didn't reply. He was too busy scrabbling about for the TV remote. Someone was coming.

"Hi," said Norm's mum from the doorway.

"Hi," said Norm's dad.

"Hi, Mum," said Norm.

"What's *what* worth, Norman?" said Norm's mum, as his dad finally located the missing remote and hit the mute button.

"This matching lacy bra and panties set for only fifteen ninety-nine!"

"Pardon?" said Norm's mum.

"I didn't say anything, Mum!" said Norm. "It was the telly! Honest!"

Norm's mum turned to look at the TV. A woman was standing, posing in her underwear. Norm instantly felt himself turning bright red. If a hole in the ground had opened up at that moment he would have quite happily jumped in it.

"Not bad!" said Norm's dad.

"Excuse me?" said Norm's mum.

"Er, I meant the price!" spluttered Norm's dad. Fifteen ninety-nine! Not bad! Not bad at all!"

"I didn't even know that's what we were watching, Mum!" said Norm.

Norm's mum didn't look convinced.

"How could you not know what you're watching, Norman?"

"I dunno, Mum," shrugged Norm. "We just weren't concentrating, were we, Dad?"

"Well we *were*," said Norm's dad. "But on other stuff."

Norm and his dad looked at each other. Was it Norm's imagination or did he detect the faintest glimmer of a smile on his dad's lips?

CHAPTER 23

Norm was out on the drive first thing the next morning. He may have just accidentally discovered his dad's darkest secret, but in the great scheme of things his dad's darkest secret really wasn't that big a deal. The only thing Norm was bothered about was seeing Chelsea again. Until he did that, she wouldn't know what stuff to order for him and where to order it from.

Everyone else had gone to IKEA. Norm had managed to wangle his way out of going with them by promising to tidy his room. Luckily, his parents hadn't actually specified *when* he should tidy his room. Norm figured that as long as he did it sometime in the next couple of years, then technically he wouldn't be breaking his promise.

"Hello, *Norman*," said Chelsea, finally appearing at the fence.

"Where have you been?" said Norm, trying not to sound as irritated as he felt.

Chelsea grinned. "Did you miss me?"

"No," said Norm flatly. "I just need to talk to you about stuff."

"Well that's funny because I need to talk to *you* about stuff too, *Norman*," said Chelsea.

"Yeah?" said Norm.

"Yeah," said Chelsea.

They eyed each other for a moment.

"Go on then," said Norm. "You first."

Chelsea eyed Norm for a moment longer. "You've been a bad boy, haven't you?"

"What do you mean?" said Norm.

"You've been telling porkies."

"What?"

"Big fat whopping porkies with a side order of fries," said Chelsea.

"What are you on about?" said Norm.

"I've been doing a bit of research."

"Have you?"

"Yeah, I have," said Chelsea, clearly relishing stringing this out as long as possible. "And guess what, *Norman*?"

"What?" said Norm.

"Turns out it's *not* actually illegal to film someone and put it on YouTube without their permission," said Chelsea.

Norm felt like he'd run slap bang into a brick wall.

"Isn't it?" he said, trying to sound surprised and failing miserably. "I thought it was."

"Well, it's not," said Chelsea. "It's perfectly legal. I've checked."

Flip, thought Norm. What did she flipping well have to go and flipping check for? That was bang out of order, that was!

"Just because something's not illegal doesn't mean you should do it," said Norm, desperately trying to regain some kind of authority.

"Uh?" said Chelsea.

"It's not actually *illegal* to snog a goat," said Norm. "Doesn't mean you should do it!"

"Are you *sure* it's not illegal?" said Chelsea. "Have you checked?"

"No," said Norm.

"Well, then," said Chelsea.

Norm was beginning to get confused.

"Look, it doesn't matter whether it's legal or not! You just can't go round filming people and putting it online without asking first!"

"Tough," said Chelsea.

"Pardon?" said Norm.

"You heard, Norman."

Chelsea was right. Norm *had* heard. He just couldn't think what to say. He could think of plenty of things he'd *like* to say – but *couldn't*. Not if he wanted Chelsea to help.

"So will you still do it?" said Norm.

"Get the stuff, you mean?" said Chelsea.

"Yeah," said Norm.

"I might."

"You *might*?"

"It'll cost you," said Chelsea.

Norm couldn't believe it. What did she mean, it would cost him? It was *already* costing him!

"How much?"

"Another ten quid," said Chelsea.

"So twenty altogether?" said Norm.

"Cash upfront," said Chelsea.

Norm sighed. He didn't have much choice.

"Here you go," he said, producing the twenty-pound note Grandpa had given him outside the betting shop.

"Cheers," said Chelsea, pocketing the money as Mikey appeared on his bike. "Chelsea *two* – Norman *nil*!"

"All right?" said Mikey, before Norm had the chance to respond.

"All right," said Norm.

"Well, look who it is!" said Chelsea. "Mr YouTube sensation himself!"

"Dunno about that," said Mikey modestly.

"What's happening, Mikey?" said Norm.

"Nothing much," said Mikey. "What was all that about?"

"What was all *what* about?" said Norm.

"Chelsea two – Norman nil?" said Mikey.

"That's me," said Chelsea.

"What's you?" said Mikey.

"I'm Chelsea."

"And don't even think about it!" said Norm.

"Don't think about what?" said Mikey.

"Making any jokes, because she's heard them all," said Norm. "And before you ask, no, she doesn't, but her dad does."

Mikey was looking more and more puzzled. "Her dad does what?"

"Supports Chelsea," said Norm. "Could've been worse though. Could've been Arsenal!"

"What on earth are you on about, Norm?" said Mikey.

"Nothing," said Norm. "I was just…"

"…trying to change the subject," interjected Chelsea. "Weren't you, *Norman*?"

"No!" snapped Norm.

Norm could feel the anger bubbling up inside him. Of *course* he was trying to change the flipping subject! The last thing he wanted was for Mikey to find out what Chelsea was going to do with his dad's money!

"He's not told you, has he?" said Chelsea to Mikey.

"Not told me what?" said Mikey.

"That he's giving me money so that I can..."

"Shut up!" yelled Norm, unable to contain his anger a second longer.

"Don't tell *me* to shut up, *Norman*!" said Chelsea. "I'm doing you a favour, remember?"

"You're not doing me a *favour*!" spat Norm. "I'm *paying* you twenty quid!"

"For what?" said Mikey.

"And you can shut up as well!" yelled Norm.

"Don't tell him to shut up!" said Chelsea.

"He's *my* flipping friend!" said Norm, indignantly. "I'll tell him to shut up if I want to!"

How *dare* she tell him not to tell Mikey to shut up, thought Norm. How flipping *dare* she? He'd got a good mind to... But before Norm had the chance to think what he had a good mind to do, a car horn beeped. They all turned round to see Mikey's dad pulling up at the end of the drive and opening his window. Mikey's mum was sat next to him. Neither seemed especially pleased to be there.

"Hi, Mikey's mum and dad!" said Norm as cheerily as possible under the circumstances.

"Home! *Now!*" said Mikey's dad to Mikey, before setting off again without so much as a glance in Norm's direction.

Norm watched as the car disappeared down the street. Mikey's dad was normally so cheerful and friendly. By his standards this was the equivalent of a full-on toddler-in-a-supermarket tantrum.

"Whoa!" said Norm. "What's up with *him*?"

"Dunno," shrugged Mikey, equally puzzled. "As far as I know they've just been shopping."

Norm had a sudden thought. "Shopping?"

Mikey nodded. "Yeah."

"Where to, Mikey?"

"Can't remember," said Mikey. "Why?"

"Nothing. Just wondering," said Norm as another car pulled up – this one containing his own parents as well as his little brothers.

"Yeah! Bikey Mikey!" shrieked Dave, tumbling out onto the pavement.

"Hi, guys," said Mikey.

"Hey guess what, Mikey?" said Brian. "We're getting a dog!"

"  " said Mikey.

"Is this your girlfriend, Norman?" said Dave, suddenly noticing Chelsea across the fence.

"No!" said Norm, emphatically.

"He *wishes*," grinned Chelsea.

"We just bumped into your parents, Mikey," said Norm's mum, lifting out a big blue IKEA carrier bag from the back of the car.

"IKEA!" blurted Mikey. "*That* was it!"

"IKEA eh?" said Norm, a horrible sinking feeling in the pit of his stomach. "What a coincidence!"

"In, Norman. *Now!*" said Norm's dad, stony-faced and heading for the front door.

"Better get home then I suppose," said Mikey, already halfway down the drive. "See you later, Norm!"

"I wouldn't bet on it," said Norm.

CHAPTER 24

Norm knew straightaway that the game was up. There was no point pretending that he had no idea what his dad was talking about. But he still did.

"Well?" said Norm's dad.

 " said Norm.

"You know perfectly well what, Norman. Let's cut straight to the chase shall we?"

Norm glanced at his mum, as if she was somehow

going to come to his rescue. But unfortunately for Norm, she wasn't.

"Your dad's right, love. Don't make things worse."

Worse? thought Norm. His plan to pimp up his bike was obviously in tatters. He may well have just seen his best friend for the last time ever. He was living in a house the size of a particularly small shoebox. How much flipping worse could things actually get?

"We know, Norman," said Norm's mum.

There was only one thing Norm's mum could possibly have been talking about. But until Norm was a hundred per cent certain, he decided to play dumb, just in case.

"Know what, Mum?"

"About the money."

"The money, Mum?" said Norm, *still* playing dumb. "What money?"

"The money you were supposed to give back to Mikey's dad."

Norm pulled a face.

"The money that Mikey's dad gave to *you* to give to *me* for the tea set?" said Norm's mum.

"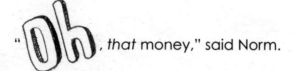, *that* money," said Norm.

"Yes, love," said Norm's mum. "*That* money."

Now that Norm was a hundred per cent certain what his mum was talking about, he decided to use delaying tactics.

"Mum, is there any chance we could talk about this later? Only I've got homework to do and you know what I'm like about leaving it till Sunday night!"

"Norman?" said Norm's dad.

"Yes, Dad?" said Norm.

"We were supposed to be cutting to the chase, remember?"

"We want to hear *your* version of events, love," said Norm's mum.

"*Now*," said Norm's dad, the vein on the side of his head beginning to throb.

Not that Norm noticed.

"Mum?" said Dave from the doorway. "Brian says he's going to..."

"Go away, Dave," said Norm's dad calmly.

"But Brian says he's going to show...."

"I said, go away!" exploded Norm's dad.

Dave promptly burst into tears and ran off, leaving Norm alone with his mum and dad.

"There was no need for that, Alan," said Norm's mum.

Just for once, thought Norm, an annoying little brother had actually come as a welcome distraction. But it was only delaying the inevitable. His parents weren't suddenly going to forget about meeting Mikey's parents in IKEA and change the subject. He was going to have to come clean sooner or later. Preferably later.

"Your dad's under pressure," explained Norm's mum.

"Tell me about it," muttered Norm.

"What was that, Norman?" said Norm's dad.

"Er, I said I'll tell you about it, Dad," said Norm.

Norm's mum and dad waited expectantly.

"Go on then," said Norm's dad.

"I didn't steal it," said Norm.

"Really?" said Norm's dad. "Well that's funny because the way I see it, that's *exactly* what you did, Norman!"

"Give him a chance to explain, Alan," said Norm's mum.

Norm sighed. Was there actually any *point* explaining?

"I borrowed it," said Norm. "I was going to pay it back."

Norm's dad snorted in derision. "Were you, now?

That's very decent of you."

Norm's mum shot Norm's dad a quick look.

"What have you done with the money, love?"

"Nothing, yet," said Norm.

"What *were* you going to do with it then?"

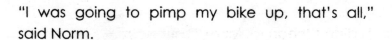

Norm thought for a moment. Would it help if he said he'd intended giving the money to charity? A home for bewildered wildebeest, or battered fish or whatever? Probably not. The bottom line was he still shouldn't have done it.

"I was going to pimp my bike up, that's all," said Norm.

"That's all?" said Norm's dad. "That's *all*?"

Norm nodded.

"What were you thinking, love?" said Norm's mum.

"He *wasn't* thinking!" said Norm's dad, before Norm had a chance to answer for himself. "Have you *any* idea how embarrassing that was, bumping into Mikey's parents in IKEA?"

Norm wasn't sure why bumping into Mikey's parents in IKEA should be anymore embarrassing than bumping into them anywhere else, but he thought it best not to say anything.

"It was..." began Norm's mum before stopping again.

"It was downright humiliating, *that's* what it was, Norman," said Norm's dad taking over.

"How could you, love?" said Norm's mum, her voice suddenly choked with emotion.

"I didn't mean to, Mum," said Norm.

"What do you mean, you didn't *mean* to?" said Norm's mum.

"It just kind of…happened," said Norm.

Norm and his dad gave each other a quick look. But not quite quick enough.

"What's going on?" said Norm's mum.

"Nothing, Mum," said Norm.

"No, really," said Norm's mum. "I saw that look. What's going on?"

"He said, *nothing*, didn't he?" snapped Norm's dad.

It was pretty clear to Norm that his dad still hadn't

told his mum about being fired.

"We need to talk," said Norm's dad.

"OK, Dad," said Norm, showing no sign of moving.

"I meant – your mum and I need to talk," said Norm's dad. "Alone."

"What? Oh right!" said Norm, twigging. "I'll, er...be off then."

Norm got up and left the room. What would Mikey be doing? he wondered. How would he react when he heard the news? How would Mikey's *parents* react if it was the other way round and Mikey had 'borrowed' a hundred pounds from his dad?

Yeah right, thought Norm, heading for the computer. Like *that* would ever happen!

CHAPTER 25

Norm pressed play and watched once again as his former best friend flew off the ramp and disappeared into the garage. At least Norm *assumed* Mikey was now officially his former best friend. He couldn't imagine Mikey's dad would let them see each other now. If Mikey actually *wanted* to see Norm in the first place of course. Which he probably didn't. Not after what Norm had done.

This was it, thought Norm. The moment it had all kicked off. If Mikey hadn't crash-landed on his mum's tea set then none of this would have happened. Because if Mikey hadn't crash landed on his mum's tea set then Mikey's dad wouldn't have given Norm the hundred pounds. End of story. But he did. And he had. And it was just the *beginning* of the story. The question was what would happen now? How would the story *end*?

Norm didn't have to wait long to find out. There was a beep from his phone. He'd got a text. It could only be from Mikey. Mikey's parents would have told him everything by now. How Norm had quite deliberately and shamelessly ripped them off. How he wasn't fit to wipe a baboon's bottom or whatever. Which was fair enough, thought Norm. They'd got a point. There was a line and Norm had definitely crossed it. The fact that he'd always meant to pay the money back was neither here nor there as far as Mikey's parents were concerned. As far as Mikey's parents were concerned Norm was nothing more than a low-down common thief.

With a certain amount of apprehension, Norm
opened up the text and read.

Steps in 10

That was it. Concise and to the point. No indication
of how Mikey was feeling. Just a simple instruction
where and when to meet. The steps at the back of
the shopping precinct in ten minutes.

Norm didn't need ten minutes. He was out the
door, on his bike and there in less than one song
on his iPod.

"You're early,"

said Mikey,
already waiting and practising his wheelies.

"I can explain everything,"
said Norm.

"There's no need."

"I didn't nick it Mikey."

"I know you didn't."

"I just borrowed it."

"I know you did."

"I'm really sorry."

"I know you are."

"If there's anything I can do..."

"There is actually."

"What?"

"You can shut up."

"What?"

"Everything's OK."

"But I'm just trying to..."

"Norm?"

"Yeah?"

"Shut up!!"

Norm looked confused.

"Everything's cool," said Mikey. "There's nothing to worry about!"

"But your dad was well hacked off," said Norm. "He never even looked at me!"

"Yeah, I know," said Mikey. "But he'd only just found out."

"So he's not mad any more then?"

"No."

This certainly wasn't what Norm had been expecting. Not that Norm was complaining.

"So, what happened?" said Norm. "In IKEA?"

"I'm not too sure," said Mikey. "All I know is that *my* mum and dad bumped into *your* mum and dad. I think your mum said thanks for the money or something but that they couldn't take it."

268

"Right," said Norm.

"So then I suppose my mum and dad would've found out that you were *meant* to give it back but that you hadn't, or something."

"Yeah, I suppose so," said Norm.

Norm still didn't fully understand. But he still wasn't complaining.

"Do they know you're here, Mikey?"

"Yeah," said Mikey.

"Meeting me?"

"Yeah," said Mikey. "I told them I was."

"So you're not, like, banned from seeing me or anything then?"

Mikey laughed. "Don't be stupid, Norm! Course I'm not!"

"I don't get it," said Norm. "My parents would've

gone ballistic if it had been the other way round."

Norm didn't know why he'd even bothered to say that. There was more chance of scientists discovering a new day of the week than there was of Mikey ever doing what *he'd* done.

Monday
Tuesday
Finarday??

"Well, I mean they obviously weren't happy at first," said Mikey. "But after a while they just calmed down. You know – kids will be kids and all that stuff?"

"But I'm not a kid any more," said Norm. "I'm nearly thirteen."

"Do you want to tell them that or shall I?" said Mikey.

They looked at each other and grinned.

It really was pretty incredible, thought Norm. How come Mikey's parents were so flipping reasonable? If it was actually possible, they'd just gone up even *further* in Norm's estimation. They were practically godlike now!

"What were you thinking, Norm?" said Mikey.

"Nothing," said Norm quickly.

"I don't mean just now," said Mikey. "I mean... what were you *thinking*?"

Norm twigged. "Oh right! You mean when..."

"Yeah."

"I wasn't," said Norm.

"What?" said Mikey.

"I *wasn't* thinking," said Norm. "It just...kind of happened."

Without another word, Mikey started to ride away. It looked like he'd said what he wanted to say and was heading home again.

"Where are you going?" said Norm.

"Nowhere," said Mikey, skidding to a halt and turning round.

Pedalling as fast as he could, Mikey flew off the top of the steps and landed perfectly at the bottom without so much as a wobble.

"Want a go, Norm?" said Mikey.

"Nah," said Norm.

"You can use my bike if you want?"

"Nah, you're all right thanks," said Norm.

Norm genuinely didn't want a go. Not because he was afraid he wouldn't be able to jump as far as Mikey, but because he still had something on his mind.

"Mikey?"

"Yeah?"

"You *do* believe me don't you?"

"Believe what?" said Mikey.

"That I was going to pay your dad back?"

"Course I do, you doughnut!" grinned Mikey.

Good old Mikey, thought Norm. Perhaps he *would* have a go at jumping the steps after all.

"Just as a matter of interest though, Norm..."

"Yeah?" said Norm.

"*How* were you going to pay it back?"

"Honestly?" said Norm.

Mikey nodded.

"Haven't got a clue," said Norm.

There was the briefest of
pauses before they
both suddenly burst
out laughing. They
laughed so loud,
they nearly didn't
hear Norm's phone
ring.

"Hello?" said Norm,
answering it.

Mikey watched as
Norm listened.

"'Kay Dad. See you soon. Bye."

Norm ended the call. He'd jump the steps another
day. It was time to go home and face the music.

CHAPTER 26

Norm was in no great hurry to get home. Whatever his parents had in store for him was unlikely to be pleasant. Whatever music he was about to face was unlikely to be to Norm's personal taste. He certainly didn't expect to be dancing.

For once, Norm was perfectly happy to get off his bike and walk up the hill. He even stopped to admire the view – a sure-fire sign that Norm was in no hurry. Norm didn't *do* views. Views were something old people banged on about, along with road works and the weather and how annoying it was when you waited ages for a bus and then three came together. But Norm knew that he couldn't delay his arrival home forever, much as he would have liked to. And anyway, his iPod needed recharging.

Norm's parents were sat side by side on the sofa when Norm eventually walked in through the door.

"Have a seat," said Norm's dad, getting straight down to business.

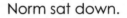

Norm sat down.

"First things first," said Norm's dad, "you go straight over and apologise and give the money back."

"But..." began Norm.

"No buts, Norman," said Norm's dad. "You're doing it."

"It won't be easy, love," said Norm's mum. "But it's the right thing to do."

Norm sighed and stood up. It *wasn't* going to be easy. In fact it might just be the hardest thing he'd ever had to do.

"Where do you think you're going?" said Norm's dad.

"To Mikey's?" said Norm.

"Sit back down. I've not finished yet."

Norm sat back down. Surely having to face Mikey's dad again was punishment enough, wasn't it? What were they going to make him do? Crawl over there on his hands and knees?

"I've been thinking," said Norm's dad.

"We both have," said Norm's mum.

"What about, Mum?" said Norm, hardly daring to ask.

"Oh, lots of things."

Lots of things? thought Norm. How *many* things? Five? *More* than five?

"The thing is..." began Norm's dad.

What was the thing? wondered Norm.

"At the end of the day..."

Which it flipping soon *would* be at this rate! thought Norm.

"We've decided..."

Norm felt like screaming. *What* had his parents decided? To seek psychiatric help? To breed budgies? To eat more cheese? Whatever it was, he wished they'd flipping well hurry up and tell him!

"...your brothers aren't the *only* ones who've found moving difficult," said Norm's mum.

"Sorry, Mum – what?" said Norm.

"We think *you've* found moving difficult as well, love."

That was what Norm had *thought* his mum had said. He just wanted to make sure.

"" said Norm.

It was all Norm *could* say. If this wasn't actually the *last* thing he'd been expecting, it was pretty near the top of the list.

"Well, you have, haven't you, Norman?" said Norm's dad.

"Erm...can't say I've really thought about it much, Dad," said Norm. "But now you come to mention it..."

"Being the oldest we thought you'd be able to cope," said Norm's mum. "But we realise now it was asking too much."

"You're still only twelve," said Norm's dad.

"Nearly thirteen," muttered Norm.

"What was that?" said Norm's dad.

"Nothing, Dad," said Norm.

"We don't think we've been giving you enough attention lately, love," said Norm's mum.

Lately? thought Norm. He hadn't been getting enough attention since Brian had been born, never mind flipping lately!

"That still doesn't excuse what you did, Norman," said Norm's dad.

Norm wanted to point out that technically he still hadn't actually *done* anything yet. Apart from not give the money back. But he hadn't actually *spent* it.

"I know, Dad," said Norm.

Several seconds passed. Several seconds that felt like several minutes to Norm.

"Are you going to tell him?" said Norm's dad eventually.

"Tell me *what*, Dad?" said Norm.

"You can tell him if you want," said Norm's mum.

"Tell me what?" said Norm, anxiously.

"No, you tell him," said Norm's dad.

"Tell me what?!" yelled Norm.

"We're going to give you the money, Norman," said Norm's mum.

"What?" said Norm.

"We're going to give you the money," said Norm's mum. "To pimp your bike up."

Norm pulled a face.

"*Give* me?"

"*Give* you," said Norm's mum.

"Not lend?"

Norm's mum shook her head.

"I don't have to pay it back?"

Norm's mum smiled. "Not unless you particularly want to, love."

Norm was doing his best to keep a lid on his emotions. He was trying not to get *too* excited. But it wasn't easy. One minute he'd been expecting to be grounded till he was at least thirty – the next he appeared to be off the hook *and* getting his bike pimped up! It was almost too much to comprehend.

"What's the catch?" said Norm.

"There's no catch," said Norm's dad.

"No terms and conditions?" said Norm.

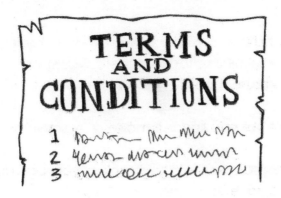

TERMS
AND
CONDITIONS

1 ~~~~~ ~~~ ~~~
2 ~~~~ ~~~~ ~~~~
3 ~~~~~ ~~~~~~

"No terms and conditions," said Norm's dad.

Norm thought for a moment. "Is this because you're buying Brian and Dave a dog?"

"Who said anything about *buying* a dog?" said Norm's mum. "We're getting one from the local dogs' home. For free!"

"Oh! Right," said Norm.

"At least we won't have to buy any dog food for a while," said Norm's dad, giving Norm's mum a meaningful look.

MEGA WOOF CHUNKS XXL

Slowly but surely Norm was allowing himself to get just a little bit excited. But there was still one thing puzzling him.

"Where will you find the money?" said Norm.

"Oh, we'll find it somewhere, love," said Norm's mum. "Don't you worry about that."

"I'll ban your mum from buying stuff off the telly," said Norm's dad. "That should save us a few quid."

"And I'll ban your dad from the computer," said Norm's mum. "That'll save us a *fortune*. Won't it, Alan?"

Norm's dad laughed nervously.

Had he *finally* told Mum about being fired then? wondered Norm. Or had his mum somehow found out herself? Either way, at that precise moment Norm could hardly have cared less. It looked like his dream of becoming World Mountain Biking Champion was well and truly back on!

"So, what do you say?" said Norm's dad.

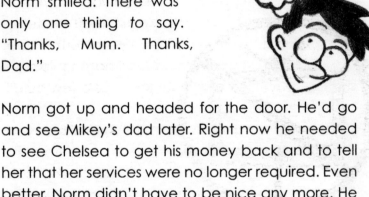

Norm smiled. There was only one thing *to* say. "Thanks, Mum. Thanks, Dad."

Norm got up and headed for the door. He'd go and see Mikey's dad later. Right now he needed to see Chelsea to get his money back and to tell her that her services were no longer required. Even better, Norm didn't have to be nice any more. He could be as horrible as he liked.

This was going to be fun, thought Norm. The only pity was that Mikey wouldn't be there to film it and post it on YouTube. *Without* Chelsea's permission!

CHAPTER 27

Much to Norm's surprise, Chelsea was huddled with Brian and Dave when he emerged from the front door. Not on her own side of the fence but on Norm's. Even more surprisingly perhaps, the three appeared to be getting on like a house on fire and sharing some kind of private joke.

"So cute!" squealed Chelsea, turning round when she heard the door slam.

"You think so?" grunted Norm. "You can have them if you want."

"She didn't mean *us*," said Brian. "She meant *you*."

"Uh?" said Norm. "What are you on about?"

"You haven't changed a bit, *Norman*!" laughed Chelsea.

It was then that Norm noticed the photo. The photo that Chelsea was holding. Norm knew straightaway which photo it was. It was the photo he'd least like Chelsea or anyone else outside of his immediate family circle to see. It was the photo guaranteed to cause maximum humiliation should it ever fall into the wrong hands. It was the photo of him and Mikey on the beach, naked as the day they were born. Admittedly, the day they were born wasn't all that many days before the photo had been taken – three or four hundred days at the most – but even so, some things were best kept private. And *this* was definitely one of them.

"Give it here!" demanded Norm, hand outstretched, marching towards Chelsea.

"I tried to warn you," said Dave.

So *that* was what Brian had said he was going to show, thought Norm, making a mental note to pay more attention to his youngest brother in future.

"Is that Mikey next to you?" said Chelsea. "It's hard to tell. He's got his back to the camera."

Norm made a grab for the photo but Chelsea swayed skilfully out of the way.

"I notice *you* haven't got *your* back to the camera, *Norman!*"

Norm made another grab for the photo, but was left clutching at thin air again.

"Oh, come on!" said Chelsea. "It's not like you can actually *see* anything!"

Chelsea paused.

"And anyway – I haven't got my magnifying glass!"

Brian and Dave both burst out laughing.

"That does it!" yelled Norm. "Give it here, or else!"

Chelsea grinned. "Else what – *Norman*?"

Norm couldn't think else what. Now that he could finally be as horrible as he liked to Chelsea, he couldn't come up with a single thing to say. It was *so* flipping unfair!

"Get off my drive!" blurted Norm.

"What? So it's illegal to stand on someone else's drive now, is it?" said Chelsea.

"Give me my money back!" said Norm.

"Why should I?" said Chelsea.

"I don't need you to do it any more."

"Do what?" said Brian.

"Shut up, Brian, you freak!"

snarled Norm. "You're for it, you are!"

"That's not a very nice thing to say to your brother," said Chelsea.

"Give me the money!" hissed Norm.

"What do you say?" said Chelsea.

"*Now!*" yelled Norm.

In a flash, Chelsea had vaulted over to her side of the fence.

"I can think of a few friends who'd like to see this!" she said, waving the photo in the air.

"Give it here!" said Norm.

"It'll cost you," said Chelsea.

"What do you mean?" said Norm.

"I get to keep the twenty pounds."

"What? No way!"

"Is that your final answer?"

"Yes, it flipping well is!" said Norm.

"In that case you leave me no alternative," said Chelsea.

Norm eyeballed Chelsea. Alternative? What alternative? What was she scheming to do now?

"As soon as I've scanned this it's going straight on Facebook."

"What?" said Norm.

"You heard."

"You wouldn't dare."

"Wouldn't I?" grinned Chelsea. "Try me. *Norman*."

"What's going on?" said Grandpa, suddenly appearing at the bottom of the drive.

"Hi, Grandpa!" sang Brian and Dave together.

"What's the problem, Norman?" said Grandpa. "Girlfriend trouble?"

Girl trouble, maybe, thought Norm. *Girlfriend* trouble? Not in a billion flipping years!

"You must be Chelsea," said Grandpa.

292

"And you must be going, Grandpa," said Norm.

"Don't worry, I'm not stopping," said Grandpa. "I've just, er…acquired a bit of money, if you know what I mean, Norman?"

Norm *did* know what Grandpa meant. He meant he'd just been to the bookies again. And won.

"And what are you going to do with it, Grandpa?" said Norm.

"I'm thinking of pampering my shed up," said Grandpa.

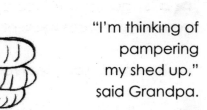

"*Pimping* it up," corrected Norm.

"Whatever," said Grandpa.

"Cool!" said Dave. "Can *we* help, Grandpa?"

"Course you can," said Grandpa.

"Yeah!" sang Brian and Dave together.

"What about you, Norman?" said Grandpa.

"What about me?" said Norm.

"You coming?"

"Nah, sorry, I can't, Grandpa," said Norm. "I'm, er...a bit busy at the moment."

"So I see," said Grandpa, his eyes crinkling ever so slightly in the corners.

"Come on then, you two."

Grandpa set off, Brian and Dave trotting happily behind him.

"Well?" said Chelsea once they'd gone.

"Well, what?" said Norm.

"Deal or no deal?"

Norm thought about it. Would Chelsea *really* put the naked baby photo up on Facebook like she'd threatened to do? It wasn't worth the risk. The consequences if she did were too horrifying to think about. And besides, Norm could easily afford to let Chelsea keep the twenty pounds now.

"Deal," said Norm.

"Very wise, *Norman*," said Chelsea.

Brian was going to pay for this, thought Norm. But not straightaway. Norm had more important things on his mind – like pimping up his bike and becoming World Mountain Biking Champion. At least *one* of those things looked like it was definitely going to happen now. The other was still more of a dream. But maybe not *quite* as distant a dream as it once was, thought Norm, staring into space and imagining himself standing on the winner's podium.

Chelsea, meanwhile, had disappeared. So too, had the naked baby photo.

Not that Norm noticed.

Read on for an exclusive sneak peek...

CHAPTER 1

Norm knew it was going to be one of those days when he woke up and found himself standing at a supermarket checkout, totally naked.

"I'm afraid that's not allowed," said the checkout assistant.

"Pardon?" said Norm.

"It's strictly against the rules," said the assistant.

"What is?" said Norm. "Shopping without any clothes on?"

"No," said the assistant. "Having ten items in your basket. This checkout's nine items or less."

Norm did a quick count. Sure enough, there were

ten items in the basket – every one of them the supermarket's own, cheaper brand.

"Sorry, I'll put one back," said Norm.

"It's too late for that," said the assistant.

"What?" said Norm, with a growing sense of disbelief.

"It's too late. I'm going to have to ask you to leave."

"Are you serious?" said Norm.

As if to demonstrate just how serious she was, the checkout assistant pushed a button and spoke into a microphone.

"Security to checkout three, please – security to checkout three."

"But..." said Norm.

"Stand away from the till," said a strangely familiar sounding voice. "You have ten seconds to comply."

Norm turned round to see a strangely familiar looking security guard approaching.

"Dad? It's me! Norman!"

But Norm's dad took no notice.

"Here, take this," he said, handing Norm a packet of own-brand coco-pops and ushering him towards the exit.

"It's OK thanks, I'm not hungry," said Norm.

"Not to eat," said Norm's dad. "To cover up your..."

"Oh, right," said Norm, suddenly remembering he was butt naked.

What was going on? wondered Norm. And why was his dad dressed as a security guard? Was he going to a fancy dress party? If so then a security guard at a supermarket was a pretty rubbish thing to go as. Unless, of course, the theme of the party was supermarkets. Or security guards. And frankly neither seemed terribly likely.

"This way please," said Norm's dad officiously.

Cameras flashed as Norm was led from the store wearing nothing but a strategically placed packet of own-brand coco pops. A crowd had gathered to watch the unfolding drama and in the distance the wail of a police siren could be heard, getting louder and louder.

"All right, Norman?" said another strangely familiar sounding voice.

Norm looked round to see Chelsea, his occasional next door neighbour, grinning from ear to ear. Worse still, she appeared to be filming proceedings with her phone. If things could actually get anymore humiliating, they just had.

"I see you've only got a small packet," laughed Chelsea.

Norm could feel himself blushing.

"How could you do this to us, Norman?" said yet another familiar sounding voice.

It was Norm's mum. Next to her, Norm could see his middle brother, Brian and next to Brian his youngest brother, Dave.

"You've brought shame on the whole family," said Norm's mum, gravely.

"No he hasn't," chirped Dave. "This is well funny, this is!"

"Shut up, Dave!" said Brian.

"Honestly, love, this is very embarrassing," said Norm's mum.

"It's not my fault, Mum!" protested Norm. "I didn't see any signs saying 'No naked shopping allowed!'"

"What?" said Norm's mum. "No, I meant it's very embarrassing you shopping in a place like this. We normally go to Tesco's. What on earth will the neighbours think?"

THE WORLD OF
NORM
Competition

Be one of the first to read the next World of Norm book!

May Cause Irritation is out in
January 2012 and we have twenty
signed copies up for grabs.
Send the answer to this question:

What does Brian call the dog he finds?

along with your name, address
and telephone number to:

World of Norm Competition
Orchard Books
338 Euston Road
London
NW1 3BH

Or email ad@hachettechildrens.co.uk

Competition will close 31st December 2011.
Only available to UK and Eire residents.
For full terms and conditions go to
www.orchardbooks.co.uk/TermsAndConditions.aspx

ORCHARD BOOKS
Celebrating 25 Years
www.orchardbooks.co.uk

GREETINGS PUNY HUMAN

This tome of staggering genius is scribed by me, the Dark Lord, a.k.a. Dirk Lloyd.

My archenemy has cast me into your world in the body of a teenager. Oh, the indignity! Brutal revenge will be mine! As soon as I've done my homework...

BUY THIS BOOK OR SUFFER THE FOLLOWING

* A period of detention in my Dungeons of Doom
* Consignment to the Rendering Vats to be turned into sausages
* Being the victim of one of my evil schemes

978 1 40831 511 8 £5.99 Pbk

THE CHOICE IS YOURS MWA HA HA!

ORCHARD BOOKS
Celebrating 25 Years
www.orchardbooks.co.uk